MAPLE TREE TALES

Marion H. Youngquist

Drurys Publishing™

MAPLE TREE TALES

First Printing

© 2006 by Marion H. Youngquist

Library of Congress Control Number: 2005937730

ISBN-13: 978-0-9770533-3-9

ISBN-10: 0-9770533-3-4

www.druryspublishing.com

KENTUCKY

Printed in the United States of America.

For our wonderful children,
Eric, Marcia, Margaret, and Mary Ellen
and
Alma Vera, our Mexican daughter

Preface

"Where do you get your stories?" Writers are often asked that question. Sometimes, a query suggests that, like the Bible, the writer lives a story before it is written. Not so. Yet situations involving friends or relatives may touch the writer's life. They may be absorbed into stories and poems without any conscious effort. Surely, Nine-Eleven – a major event – changed the author's life as it did many people. It is reflected in this book through an imaginative story.

An observant writer finds stories in many places. Conversations are overheard in restaurants, in airport lounges or the supermarket check-out line. One-sided remarks on a cell phone can spark the imagination. These comments may be jotted into a little notebook, carried in the writer's pocket, and used years later.

Many people are uncertain troubled souls who have difficulty living full and complete lives. Some are like rocks skipped across a pond. Before a rock sinks, tiny circles mark each hit. The water flows on, but a leaf may be trapped, spinning in a whirlpool. Or a small stick is pushed into another current. Each one seems powerless to change direction. So it seems with people.

Maple Tree Tales are interrelated stories of people in Whittimore, a town somewhere in the USA. Many young people complain that nothing ever happens there. In their immaturity, they do not understand constantly changing relationships. The historic Sugar Maple witnesses many events. It continues to watch the generations who pass by.

Wisdom belongs to the perceptive observer. Someone has said, *To those who feel, life is a tragedy . . . to those to think, life is a comedy.*

Thank you . . . to my husband Ted and our daughter Margaret Fleming, and good friends Sue Romo, Ruby Hauch and Grace Gunnlaugsson for manuscript help.
A special *Thank You* to Gary Drury and the staff at Drury's Publishing in Hodgenville, Kentucky for encouragement and acceptance of these stories.

Marion Neal Horn Youngquist
Wauwatosa, Wisconsin

TABLE OF CONTENTS

All characters and stories are fictitious.

Apology

Near the historic Sugar Maple
and the blacktopped sprawl of suburbia
and shopping malls,
crabgrass multiplies
and barbecues sizzle,
while deck posts rot
and TVs blare—
here are uncertain troubled souls,
their legacy
a three-car garage
and a thousand tossed pop cans.

—mhy

Inspired by T.S. Eliot and his fine poem,
The Wasteland

Autumn Maple

The elderly maple has seen
many years but this autumn his
metamorphosis will be remembered
as many stop to watch his evolution
from mint green leaves into brilliant
fall foliage which takes away any
passerby's breath, the way his ever
graceful leaves fall gently to the
ground to blanket the grass
with a rainbow coat
chestnut
flame
gold
rust
ocher
scarlet
crimson
as the season turns he will become bare and
charcoal gray until spring rescues him once more.

— Rebecca Nicole Neal Fleming
Grand-daughter, 13 years old

Autumn Dancer

Sugar Maple dons
her flamenco gown shimmers
in the breeze she swishes her dress
scarlet taffeta with glints of gold
she rustles sways to an autumn air tempo
in a dreamy dance suddenly she swirls
twirls bows low castanets clicking faster
and faster caught by a frenzied whirlwind
she flings off her gown falls away
in a russet heap at her feet reveals
her gnarled limbs twisted body
nakedness
etched
against
a dull
gray sky
She stands alone abandoned
until the kindly Snow King wraps her in ermine.

– Marion Neal Horn Youngquist

THE SUGAR MAPLE

On Pioneer Drive, a Sugar Maple stands at a curve. Some believe that as a sapling, it marked an early Native American trail—later to become a road followed by pioneer wagons on their westward journey. Through the years the tree grew larger. Now its great trunk holds many rings that recorded the growth of a city, sprawling in all directions.

Pioneer Drive enters the town from the east, out near Old Fort Whittimore Square. That was always a misnomer because Fort Whittimore was a trading post, founded by Isaiah Whittimore when he settled in the region. Some claimed he crossed the Delaware with General Washington on that bitter Christmas Eve in 1776. Others said that he argued in Philadelphia with Ben Franklin that every territory ought to be sovereign. Whatever the truth, Isaiah went west to trade with the Indians, married a squaw and hurried the wagon trains along, so that his area would remain sparsely settled.

When Jacob Mueller built a flour mill by Beaver River, Isaiah said the land was too crowded. Then Levi Morrison opened a dry-goods store, and Silas Ward followed with a blacksmith shop. After the Union Pacific surveyed for railroad tracks, a station was built away from the river. Someone put up a sign *Whittimore Junction* without even asking Isaiah. He shook his head—his long beard grizzled like other aged trappers. He knew that his control was gone. He barred the Fort's doors and quit buying furs. He saw a village springing up around the railroad station, two miles west of his fort.

A circuit riding Methodist preacher, the Reverend Wesley Warren established First Methodist Church, soon to be followed by Presbyterians, who met upstairs over the drug store. When they built, the Masonic brothers rented the space and later put up a cream brick hall across from the new red brick Carnegie Library with its Roman arch over the front door—just like the one on the state capitol. Some Free-Will Baptists bought land near Beaver River and held revival meetings in a tent. Whittimore citizens and those on surrounding farms firmly believed in the providence of the Almighty God, the Golden Rule and clean living. Such a prosperous place proved they were a chosen people.

Many citizens petitioned for Whittimore Junction to be the county seat. Jacob, Levi and Silas were leaders who persuaded the Central State Bank to open a branch. The fine new bank boasted Greek columns in front and bronze grillwork at the counter. Horace Cooper arrived from Independence, Missouri to be the first bank president. His wife Lydia quickly persuaded him to drop *Junction* from the bank's letterhead. She said "It sounds so rural. What will our friends in St. Louis think. . . that we've come to some wilderness crossroads?"

When the next map was printed, Whittimore was marked with a circle as the county seat of Franklin County. A two-story courthouse was erected on a central square. Judge Joseph Boggs, appointed magistrate, arrived with two spinster daughters. Miss Lavinia hung a shingle in the living room window, *French Dressmaker*, which meant that she ordered Paris patterns from New York. Her sister Rose also hung a sign below–*Music Teacher*. She played the organ for forty years at the First Methodist Church. That only ended when she fell off the bench at a Wednesday night choir practice—her long service noted at her funeral three days later.

Whittimore drew sturdy immigrants like the Norwegians who settled in the valley north of Whittimore. The Johnsons and Trovattens each gave adjoining parcels for St. Olaf Lutheran Church and a cemetery, located beside *Lake Bergen* which they so-named. When the state maps arrived, the printer had left out the *g* so ever after it was called *Lake Beren*. The church was white-frame with a pump organ ordered from Philadelphia. It cost almost as much as the church, as all the Johnsons would proudly explain. The Trovattens thought the organ was extravagant. What the congregation needed was a pastor with a good voice to lead them in plain singing. When Pastor Erwin Syzerud and his wife Ione arrived from Hamar, the Johnsons felt affirmed. His wife played the organ and could also direct a choir. Many prayers of thanksgiving were said. The Trovattens didn't leave the congregation, because sixteen year-old Signe Trovatten was asked to sing *Den Store Hvide Flok* at all the funerals.

Polish immigrants settled on the southern hills and erected St. Mary's brick church, on a high point. It was a cream-colored building with walnut pews and a stained glass window made in Chicago. Quickly, they envisioned a school and perhaps, even a seminary spreading across the hilltop. Their church steeple could be seen for miles. They were surprised when the Archbishop sent a ruddy Irishman, Father Michael O'Reilly, as their priest. He enjoyed lots of their prune kolaches and didn't miss Irish soda bread a bit. He ate sauerkraut and Polish sausage with gusto, so parishioners came to love him, even if he was a bit tipsy after Sunday masses.

The Maple Tree knew the farmers by the clip-clop of their horses when they came to town each Wednesday afternoon and Saturday morning. A few daughters were lucky to find places to work for room and board while they attended the brand new high school, complete with a chemistry room for

James Woodrow, the math and science teacher. Signe Trovatten and Maria Zielinski enrolled, the first girl in either family to be educated. They worked for their room-and-board at Bertha Schultz's Boarding House. Her husband, Dutch, opened a saloon two blocks away. Sometimes the girls had to deliver bread and rolls to the saloon. They stepped in cautiously with their deliveries and carried back a money pouch for Bertha to deposit. The two girls shared a cold third story bedroom. A carved wooden cross hung above Signe's bed and a crucifix stood on Maria's night table. So protected, the girls became good friends that lasted their lifetimes—even when Signe took a three-month course at Professor Hiram Beardsley's Normal School and Maria got married that same summer.

Beardsley's Normal School lasted eight years until the building burned one night when the Professor dropped his pipe in a wastebasket. After the Civil War, he left for a new college out west, leaving an unpaid bill at the Polish Diner. However, Whittimore met the challenge. Its young citizens were not to be deprived of a higher education. Through the efforts of Horace Cooper and Levi Morrison, Sr., an advertisement was placed in a Boston paper. For twenty-five thousand dollars, an educational institution would be named for the donor in the thriving town of Whittimore. In Boston, Cyrus McNaughton, president of the Fine Shoe factory (*Fine Shoes to Fit your Feet*), wrote the check and never visited his college.

Horace was surprised when that old bachelor Axel Fuhrmeister proposed to deed his eighty-acre farm to the college if he could stay in his log cabin until death and be buried beside it. The farm was wooded, high above Beaver River. Axel signed the deed with an X. No one expected him to live for thirty more years—until he was ninety-three. A spruce windbreak shielded the coeds from his cabin, outhouse and his odd habits—going shirtless or playing his harmonica to laying hens. His old barn was torn down when a Fieldhouse was built. His cabin and burial plot are listed on the state Historical Register.

Both McNaughton Hall with offices and classrooms and Fuhrmeister Hall, the coed dormitory, were built the first year. Dr. Silas Warwick from Yale was hired as President. Known for his essays on Shakespeare, he also brought along a collection of North American stuffed birds. He persuaded Horace and Lydia Cooper to endow the library. The Morrison Science building followed, along with the Lincoln Men's dormitory to honor the late President. McNaughton College was called a *western Yale*.

The Washington Hotel and the Opera House were finished the same year that Sarah Bernhardt made her second American tour. She played *La Dame aux camellias* and left a fan and lace shawl. These are proudly displayed in her dressing room, preserved by the Franklin County Historical Society and recognized on their monthly tours.

Whittimore merchants organized the Chamber of Commerce just before the Wall Street Crash in October of '29. Not much happened until Levi Morrison, Jr. persuaded the merchants to create an Industrial Park on the south side. He spearheaded a campaign *Whittimore On The Move* to entice light industry. WOTM calendars and notepads were everywhere. Finally, a small electrical appliance company erected the first glass and steel building in the park. People admired the functional design. A chocolate factory followed. Two major employers meant the Depression was over. Better times were ahead.

Pioneer Drive cuts the city in half, passes the county courthouse and crosses Main Street—now revitalized as a cobblestone walking street where boutiques, cafes and banks cluster. Lawyers and insurance salesmen moved into upscale offices in the old Mueller Flour Mill. Two malls opened—East Plaza and Westside. Old home-owned department stores, like Morrison's, are gone. People attend concerts and plays in the restored Opera House. The Polish Diner and Norwegian Bakery are gone, but there are two Chinese carry-outs and a Mexican place. Schulz Saloon became the Black Forest Inn—later bought by a pizza chain.

Each change was observed by the Sugar Maple. It grew larger with every passing year. Beyond the curve, the first subdivision was built after World War II. Sturdy brick–and–stone homes were located along a grid of straight streets. They were a three bedroom ranch-style with a living room and dining ell, plus an eat-in kitchen. Many G.I.s came home from Europe or the Pacific, or later Korea, to marry their sweethearts and buy their dream homes. Some still live there, keeping their lawns neatly mowed in summer and their driveways shoveled in winter.

For many aging couples, the Sugar Maple is the landmark that tells them they will soon be home. They watch for the first green leaves of spring with a satisfied joy that they are alive for another year. Ordered by a physician at an HMO clinic to walk for exercise, they pause beneath the tree on a summer evening and refuse to admit that they're too tired to go further. In the fall they stop their car to admire the fiery display of scarlet, gold and rust leaves—fearing that perhaps this is their last autumn. In winter they watch the stark branches etched against a gray sky and comment that it's like a Homer painting.

Hostesses use the Sugar Maple as a reference point to give directions to their large places in Windsor Estates or Knollwood Acres which cover the western hills. They will say, "Come west, two miles from the Maple on Pioneer Drive. Turn left . . . " The guest will know how to get there.

Other trees along the old Pioneer trail were cut down long ago when it was called Pioneer Road. Later it was widened for horseless carriages. A City Council changed Road to Drive after the war to give it a more modern sound. Through all the changes, the Sugar Maple remained—a silent sentinel and witness to events around it.

Within its heart, the Sugar Maple holds secrets. Once, a century ago, children waited at the tree until stragglers could walk with them to a one-room schoolhouse. Initials were carved on the trunk, but those knifing the tree are long dead. Now the tree bark barely registers their mark. One student went east to Yale. He became a research scientist and developed a vaccine that has been beneficial across the world. Another was a well-know writer of quaint children's stories, enjoyed at firesides along with McGuffey's Reader.

One time—near the century's end—a horse-and-buggy stopped beneath the tree in the August moonlight so a courting couple could pledge their love forever. Now their great-grandchildren track genealogies, but none know or will discover the part that the Maple tree played in their family history.

When farmers drove their milk wagons to town, they watched the wind whip through the Maple's leaves. They realized a storm was coming—a warning to bring their animals into their barns. Sometimes, they paused beneath its shade and socialized with another farmer while their horses rested. The Maple tree was a weatherman and a silent friend.

Does the Sugar Maple know how lives will be forever changed by its presence tonight? Some will drive by and say, "Oh that's where it happened." Days will roll into months and then into years. The event will become a memory to only a few. However, a curious aftermath will follow—like a slashed rope whose fibers fray in all directions and can never be made whole again.

A worried young man leaves a downtown bank late on a winter afternoon. It's already dusk. He hunches up his black leather jacket and pulls up the collar around his thin neck. His name is *Eddie* and he's almost thirty. He's lean-looking, pale and gaunt. Lines form deep furrows between his eyebrows. He's unsure about what to do because he needs money. This second bank has turned down his loan application.

He's already asked his parents for money. His mother bit a lower lip before asking questions about his salary and how much was his credit card debt? His father raised his eyebrows and sighed, "No one in our family ever filed for bankruptcy. There must be some way . . ." They didn't give him a loan, so he approached the second bank.

Eddie is not a drinker, but he stops at Harry's Pub and Grill. He needs time before he faces Ginger, his wife. She wants a basement den with a big TV screen for their two kids. He's argued that Taylor and Tyler are only four and two. They don't need a den now. The kids have a new gym and swing set in the backyard, a custom-built one. That was another equity loan.

He knows Ginger wants a perfect house. She cuts pictures out of slick magazines to show him how their two-bedroom ranch could be redone. Do real people live in those perfect rooms with their marble floors and glass showers? She doesn't grasp that loans have to be repaid. They can't be deferred, no matter what the TV finance companies advertise.

A woman—a stranger—sits close by, talking to the bartender. She turns to Eddie. "You look like you lost a friend."

"Things are rough. I'm going broke." Eddie signals, "A coke, please."

She looks at his glass. "You need something stronger than that." She turns to the bartender. "Fix him up . . . Vodka with a twist. Put it on my tab."

Eddie smiles at her. The woman has frizzy gray hair and scarlet lips. On her hands are several glittering rings. She's old enough to be his mother. He'd like to talk to her, but he's afraid because he'd have to buy her a drink in return. He sits there, sipping his drink, adjusting to the liquor. People around him are laughing. The music is loud with a bongo beat. Although he felt alone before, now he senses comfort—acceptance—belonging. He leans back and relaxes.

He recalls his high school years. They had been miserable because he lacked talent in anything. When he tried out for a team, he was thin and often winded after practice. Classes were boring. The only time he really felt good was behind the wheel of his Dad's car. That's why his delivery job—the union pay—the health benefits—had been the first good thing in his life.

Then he met Ginger. When he delivered supplies to the House of Beauty School, Ginger was there, behind the reception desk every Tuesday as part of her training. She was the only girl who ever flirted with him

Eddie orders another drink.

He knows his delivery job doesn't cover expenses anymore. Ginger is always after him about their house. She doesn't like the ranch. Even if the kids are small, she wants each to have a bedroom. What will Ginger say when he tells her that the second bank has turned them down?

Eddie orders another drink.

He carefully thinks about what he'll say. "Our papers aren't in order. It takes a month before they will consider a new loan." Now it's harder to find reasons.

Eddie orders another drink.

It's easy to swallow the liquid. He feels warm—warmer than he has for a long time. Maybe his Mom and Dad really didn't understand his situation. Maybe he should try them again. He doesn't remember if they really turned him down. It isn't too late. Yes, that's it. Go back home to Mom and Dad.

"Bartender, I need one for the road."

"Are you sure? Haven't you had enough?" the bartender replies. He pushes across a glass mainly filled with sparkling ice cubes.

Eddie rises and walks with deliberate steps as he makes his way to the door. The cold air outside hits him. He feels splashes of rain on his face. He stumbles when he opens the door and climbs into his car. He fumbles with the key and drives slowly toward Pioneer Drive. He stays focused on the yellow line. Other cars make a wide arc and honk at him. He is unaware of them.

He picks up speed as he thinks of his parents—always so willing to help. Yes, he can't wait to get there. He feels a surge of power in his hands as the car leaps forward. The road becomes darker and darker. The streetlights seem distant—little yellow moons high in the sky. The rain distorts the headlights of oncoming traffic. Cars veer around him. He tries to grasp the wiper control. Where is the defroster? Suddenly, there is a curve. The Sugar Maple looms large in his headlights. He tries to swerve. The car crumples on impact. Eddie is crushed beneath the wheel. Dead.

Many lives are touched by the accident at the Sugar Maple that night.

At midnight, a policeman gives the young widow Ginger his sad report of Eddie's accident. Someday, the officer will puzzle over Ginger's familiar face. Did he stop her for a traffic violation? Was she stranded somewhere?

Eddie's parents, Irma and Henry, see a news flash about an accident on Pioneer Drive—details pending. They go to bed, unaware of their loss.

A middle-aged woman spreads out her night creams—their pastel contents like glowing pearls to enhance her youthful appearance, which nothing must destroy.

Across town, a salesman and his wife watch the nightly news, aware that their nine-year-old son Buddy is restless again tonight and won't settle down.

There are others—people across state lines who will

indirectly be affected.

The Maple tree's knowledge seems as wide as its spreading branches. After that fateful night, each new ring will mark changes as it grows larger during the next two decades. Listen to it whisper in the night wind. Hear the secrets held within its heart.

GINGER'S HOROSCOPE

When The Times came that morning, Ginger hurriedly turned to Angela's Star Horoscope. There in black-and-white was the help she needed.

"Don't let unexpected events frazzle your nerves. If in doubt, bolster your self-confidence. You're on a winning Streak."

Breakfast was chaotic. Taylor wanted her fingernails painted purple for some kid's birthday celebration at school. Tyler spilled cereal and crunched it underfoot. Last night Stewie promised that he would ask his wife Connie for a divorce. He didn't call back. She fell asleep after the Tonight show ended. The TV played all night until she awakened at five a.m. and switched it off.

This would not be a good morning. Her Aries horoscope was right—her nerves were frazzled.

She piled Taylor and Tyler in the van and dropped them off at school. As she drove back along Pioneer Drive, she noticed the old Sugar Maple. Gold and rust leaves barely clung to the branches. That was where Eddie died—dear Eddie who never made enough money, but he was real sweet and wanted to give her everything. If he had lived, she'd never have given Stewie a second glance, but what's a widow to do? Never have any fun?

Eddie had died over two years ago. Sometimes, it seemed like yesterday. She still remembered the horoscope for that awful day—"Changes are ahead and not everything will go your way." She had to accept that Eddie's fate was in the stars.

Ginger parked the car where she could look at the Sugar Maple. That tree had changed her whole life. It left her—not even twenty-five—with two kids, but no husband. Then she met Stewie. Yesterday he told her to hang on a little longer. He was so sure his wife would give him a divorce.

Her future seemed odd, sad and scary—like Eddie's death. She wished she could talk to someone like a mother or a good friend—someone who would understand. She remembered it all—like it happened yesterday. Ginger leaned back and closed her eyes. Eddie told her he would be back after he talked to his folks. Instead he died.

Eddie, I was Cinderella and you were my Prince while it lasted.

You looked so great in your brown-and-tan uniform with the brass buttons. You delivered supplies to the House of Beauty School. I worked the desk every Tuesday when you made your stop. You were cute when you lifted your eyebrow and winked. I flirted back, until you asked me out. You ordered me a Shirley Temple because I was only seventeen. You wouldn't let me taste your drink. Then I found out you had a coke. You sure took care of me. I remember everything.

When I met your parents, Irma and Henry, I even flirted a little with your old man—hugged him once and cooed in his ear, "I'll bet you were REALLY GOOD-LOOKING in your Marine uniform. I love those blue jackets with the red trim." He turned a little red, but smiled like he was pleased.

Irma, your Mom, fixed a real nice dinner of chicken-and-dumplings. We ate in your sunny dining room with a smooth white tablecloth, ironed real good. I was afraid to touch it. My hands shook as I took some dumplings. I was scared of spilling gravy on all that whiteness. We ate like real people that day.

Irma asked, "Where do your parents live?"

I freaked out. I couldn't tell the truth—that my Dad was a gambler who disappeared years ago. My Mom spent a year in jail for drugs and took off for Biloxi when she got out. I lived in a foster home until I got my GED. I cleaned rooms at a motel to get money for beauty school.

I lowered my eyes—like I was real sad—and said, "My father died in a railroad accident. He was an engineer."

"How tragic," Irma replied.

"My mother is down south. She helps my aunt run a bed-and-breakfast. A real high-class place." Irma looked at me strangely so I quickly changed the subject. "Maybe you could teach me how to make dumplings."

That pleased Irma. She passed the dish again. Although I thought that the dumplings were rather gummy, I took two more helpings. I didn't want any more questions. I got us out of there real fast with an excuse that I had to study for an exam.

Oh, I wanted to get married more than anything! Remember, how we eloped—went to Las Vegas before your parents could object? Sometimes they bug me now about seeing Taylor and Tyler every week. My horoscope said "Keep relationships healthy, so that you have assistance when you need it." I do take the kids over to their place when I get real busy. They get a puzzled look when I tell them how well I'm doing, but they don't know about Stewie yet.

You know how religious Irma and Henry are—long-time members of St. John or St. James—or whatever saint's inside. You said the building was Old Gothic with a real fancy altar and a big heavy gold cross hanging from way up high. Why does Irma call that round stained glass window *a rose window*? I've looked ever so many times and never found any roses in it.

They had their old pastor do your funeral. He talked about how good God is, how everyone can trust God to take care of their loved ones. I sat there crying real hard, because I was scared about raising two kids alone. You were a real good Daddy and helped a lot. You gave the kids their baths and put them to bed each night.

Your parents were shocked at the funeral when I spoke up to the pastor. "What kind of a loving God kills the Daddy of my two kids and leaves me to raise them alone?"

Irma turned to the minister. "Ginger's upset. I'm sure that she doesn't mean what she says."

"I do! I do!" I kept on. "God's unfair! And don't tell me that kids are a gift from God. Eddie and I knew where babies come from. We didn't need any help from God!"

Irma looked like she'd have a heart attack and die right there. The preacher almost had two funerals for the price of one. It was the wrong thing to say, but I saw trouble ahead.

Irma and Henry paid for the funeral lunch. The church ladies put on a big spread of ham, potato salad, coleslaw, fruit salad and three kinds of cake. Church people think that food's a cure-all. Doesn't matter–rain or shine–they eat.

Irma took some citrus salad and said, "I couldn't go through Edward's death without the help of the Lord."

I made a face. "Well, HE can SEND SOME my way. I've got two kids to raise."

"Now, Ginger, your two little angels are a gift from God," a church lady interrupted, pouring coffee.

I'd heard that line before, so I said straight out, "Not mine! Two trips to Las Vegas. Two lucky nights at the slots. Two lucky nights in bed!"

Old Coffee-Pot lady went back to the kitchen laughing. Maybe she thought I was joking.

Irma was flustered and patted my shoulder. "We'll help with the grandchildren. Edward would want us to do that much. We want to keep busy or the sadness will be too much to bear."

"Don't worry about us. I read my horoscope today. It said, *Not everything will be easy. Be wary of advice.*" I said that last part slowly so she'd understand. I didn't want her telling me what to do.

"You have to do what you think is best."

"And don't ask questions," I continued. "You snoop around—how much did the cedar deck cost? Why did I want new birch cabinets in the kitchen? It was none or your business what we spent. And another thing—Eddie bought that ranch house because you called it a *darling little place*. I want a better address, and you can keep your mouth shut."

"Please, Ginger, let's not say things we regret. Edward asked us for a loan. He made a good salary. We couldn't understand why he needed more money. So we did ask questions."

"From the start, you never liked me."

"That's not true."

"It's not my fault if Eddie got drunk and wrapped himself around a tree. I can't sue the car dealer, or hospital or anyone and get anything. I'm the one stuck in that little house with two kids."

Your Mom just stared at me and said in a small voice, "I feel so sorry for you."

I slammed the door on the whole world. I was ALONE again. Just like when I went to beauty school, and my Mom went down south. She never came to your funeral. She never called or asked how I'm doing. Never.

Well, my life changed around in a hurry. I was really surprised that you left a lot of insurance. Your folks had seen to that. It almost made me get religion and believe in God. I bought a two-story Cape Cod on a nice street. I wanted to put a beauty shop in the basement, but city codes didn't allow that. I gave up and made it into a playroom with cutouts of Mickey Mouse and Cinderella. It looks real cute.

A year passed. I got the new house furnished by a saleslady at the mall. One night I realized I was in bed alone. That was no fun. It was time for a new guy in my life. I knew Irma and Henry watched me, but I figured that if I'd died and gone to heaven (that's a laugh) you'd have been on the move in three months.

Bills piled up. I wanted our kids to have things I never had. One morning my horoscope read If problems arise, seek professional help. I went to a financial counselor. That woman said straight out that I had to stop spending money or get a job to pay for my extras. Imagine that! She suggested a temp agency. So I figured I'd take something downtown where the money and men are. Right away, I got hired to fill in for a receptionist who was on maternity leave. My job was for three months. Irma and Henry agreed to watch the kids after school. I took off my wedding ring.

I met Stewie at Christmastime. After work a group went to the Carousel Room—high up where we could see the city lights. The scene was lovely with big red and green holiday wreaths. Even the dirty snow looked nice. A pianist jazzed some old show tunes.

I had on my new diamond earrings (I know you would want me to have them) and that curvy black dress that always gets a glance. After a second martini, I felt relaxed and happy. I wished the party would last all night. I knew that something good would happen because my horoscope said, "Hard work will bring a reward, but may add responsibility." I wanted my hard work to bring something good—like a new guy.

I turned around and almost spilled my drink. There was Stewie.

He said, "I don't think we've met. I'm Stewart—in Sales. My friends call me Stew."

"I'm Ginger . . . a temp. Receptionist . . . third floor." I paused. "I think I'll call you Stewie."

"Call me anything you like—just call," he grinned.

"You call first."

"Maybe I will." Stewie looked at my left hand. "How come you're not married?"

"I'm a widow. My husband died in an accident over two years ago."

Stewie held me at arm's length. "In that black dress you're very dangerous . . . like a black widow spider."

"I don't bite."

" . . . Or maybe a cute black furry kitten."

"It's up to you to find out what I am."

"Is that a challenge?" he asked with raised eyebrows.

"I don't play games. I play for real." I walked away. I knew he would follow me.

Stewie looked really good. His hair was full with a comb-out over a bald spot. He was a little stocky. His suit had a silky sheen. I felt vibes between us right away. We sat at the same table. My leg brushed his a couple of times. Simpatico—know what I mean? Stewie made sure I was on his United Way team. That meant we could lunch together. I asked about mutual funds, so Stewie dropped by my place with some brochures and stayed awhile. He suggested an Index Fund and a Growth thing. That's what I like about married men. They know how to take care of a woman.

Stewie didn't make a move, but I did. One Saturday morning I read my horoscope that advised. "Believe in your abilities. Put your hidden assets to work." It was for a Taurus, but it really fit me, so what the heck?

I sent the kids to Irma and Henry for the week-end, so they could take them to Sunday School. They asked me to go with them and see the Light, too. What I needed was a fun time. You always said that we should cut loose sometimes—that God made us that way. I took your advice.

Stewie dropped by to help with my tax return. I got tired of numbers and said, "Let's take a break. Would you like to see my house?"

We went upstairs. He admired the lilac hedge from my bedroom window.

"I love the smell of lilacs," I sighed. I sat on the bed and smoothed the spread. "It's been a long time since I've had any fun in my life."

Stewie stared a minute and sat beside me. He gave me a crooked little smile. "Well, let's remedy that."

It was all in the stars because the Gemini horoscope said that morning to "Stay focused. Explain to your lover how much you care." That fit me, too.

His wife Connie found out about our Saturday together. She got mad. She called me late one night and yelled that Stewie can't be trusted–that he's had other affairs. I know that I can handle him better than she did.

Eddie, I want you to understand how it all happened. Stewie will be a perfect husband, because I understand men. I know what they want. I've read a lot of paperbacks, so I know a lot about love, too.

I'm an Aries. This morning my horoscope said "You're on a winning streak."

I sure am.

BIRTHDAY PRESENT

As Kitt signed the delivery slip for a dozen long-stemmed red roses, she thought, *This will be a very good birthday. Leon sends me flowers and I'm having lunch with our daughter Connie.*

As she passed the hall mirror, she stopped and patted her sleek ash blonde hair. She leaned closer to study her smooth taut skin. Like good hair coloring, plastic surgery was worth the cost. The expensive night creams helped, too. Her skin was free of any line. She was past fifty, but she knew she looked younger. Someone asked in the Glenbrook Country Club grill if she were Leon's trophy wife.

When the phone rang, Connie began to sing-song the lines "Happy Birthday . . . dear Mother." Then she giggled nervously, "I want to be the first to wish you a great day."

Connie's early call surprised Kitt. "Thanks. I'm glad for the song now, and not in the restaurant. No one needs to be reminded of birthdays when you're over fifty."

This wasn't true. Kitt knew she was proud of her youthful looks. In fact, it was a thrill to see people surprised when she introduced Connie as her daughter. It was not unusual to be mistaken for Connie's sister when they were together. Kitt thought, Connie is only in her mid-thirties. Already she has a few gray hairs at her temples. Connie really ought to go to a salon soon.

Connie paused, "I can't make lunch today."

"Oh, Connie, you promised!" Kitt protested. "We planned this because you and Stewart and Buddy couldn't come last

Sunday for an early celebration."

Lately, Connie always found lame excuses—Buddy had a soccer practice or Stewart was in a golf tourney. Finally, she agreed to the midweek luncheon date with her mother. Kitt was relieved. Maybe it was better to celebrate alone with Connie.

Connie was silent. She sighed, "I'm a substitute den mother. Buddy's Cub Scouts will meet here after school. I can't linger over lunch."

"Surely, you can spend an hour with me." Kitt tried to hide her disappointment. "We'll meet at that new place The Toledo." Actually, it was near Stewart's office, but he was off on a marketing trip. Atlanta? Houston? Connie was evasive. "The Times says it's rather dark, but very good food." Connie didn't respond. "You like Mexican food, although the menu is a more Spanish cuisine than . . . "

There was a long pause. Finally, Connie answered, "Okay, but I can't make it until twelve. I have an appointment this morning."

Kitt replaced the phone, puzzled about Connie's attitude. What caused her resistance to a simple luncheon date? Things did seem a bit different since Connie and Stewart had returned from their Maui vacation two months ago. Kitt remembered how little frowns quickly crossed Connie's brow. Sometimes, she bit her lip as if she had a secret. And Buddy was so quiet while his parents were gone. Even Leon noticed how seldom Buddy laughed, but then their grandson was glued to TV or electronic games.

Kitt poured herself a large glass of carrot juice. Two months? Then it hit her! Connie was having a baby! Did Connie avoid Sunday dinner and their luncheon date because of morning nausea? Of course! Kitt surmised that Connie's appointment that day was at the OB clinic.

Now, Kitt felt guilty over her irritation with Connie. She would play along and never confess that she had guessed

Connie's secret. Kitt hoped Connie would have a baby girl. Buddy was a fine grandson, but Kitt never felt she connected with him. For one thing, he called her *Grandma* when she asked to be called *Nana*. A granddaughter would follow her wishes. She smiled in the mirror. Was it even possible that she would be taken for her granddaughter's mother as she pushed a stroller through the park? Some forty-something professional women gave up careers for motherhood. Kitt realized how valuable her exercise routine was to keep her body slim and trim—to look young and vital.

Maybe Connie won't tell me until she's over her nausea, but a new baby is a wonderful birthday present. Oh, she must!

Kitt dressed carefully for the expected announcement. She needed something casual, like Connie might wear. She donned beige slacks with a muted jacket and bright scarf. She drove past the Sugar Maple and thought it was the most colorful ever—brilliant scarlet and gold leaves still with a touch of green. Autumn was a time of harvest when all good things come together. It was the same with her life. At her last class reunion, she was envied by other women for her youthful appearance.

Kitt pulled into a Toledo parking space. She would get a table and not delay Connie. She stepped into the dark lobby with dim sconces along the wall. Five people crowded around a brassy blonde hostess with a black lace mantilla who stood in the spotlight, taking reservations. Finally, Kitt reached her.

"There's a twenty-minute wait," the hostess said. "First name?"

"Kitt . . . a reservation for two."

"You can wait in the bar."

Kitt declined and sat down on a bench in the semi-darkness. Others arrived, filling the entrance. The dining room would be crowded—a sign of a good restaurant. Kitt relaxed.

The hostess called out in a breathy voice, "Stewie, party of two . . . Stewie, party of two . . . "

Kitt lifted her head to see someone with a similar nickname to Connie's husband. She gasped. Stewart stood in the spotlight with his arm pressed around the waist of an auburn-haired woman who looked up at him with adoring eyes. He leaned over and whispered in her ear, then straightened up as a waiter led the couple into the dining room. They were laughing, and he kept his arm around her.

Kitt jumped up and pushed against the heavy door. She felt a rush of autumn air. She thought *I can't let Connie know that I've seen Stewart with another woman. I must protect Connie . . . in her condition.*

She saw Connie walk quickly toward her. Instinctively, Kitt reached out for a hug and brushed Connie's cheek with a kiss.

"I don't want to eat here," Kitt said. "It's too dark, and the menu isn't very good. It's my birthday. I can eat where I please."

Connie took Kitt's arm protectively, as if she were the parent. She steered Kitt to a back parking lot. There Connie pointed out Stewart's red sports car. "You saw Stew inside, didn't you? We've got a lot to talk about. Leave your car here. Pick it up later. There's a country restaurant down the road."

Kitt said, "I really don't feel like eating. I'll go home."

"It's best," Connie agreed. "I don't feel like eating either. I just came from the lawyer's office. He's filing my divorce papers next Monday."

"That soon? Maybe you should wait. Try to work things out."

"The Maui trip didn't work things out. Stew phoned this latest girl friend every day. He went deep-sea fishing by himself. I read books and sunned alone."

"Divorce isn't the answer," Kitt replied. She believed

that. She had lived by that and was still married in spite of Leon's career, his expensive taste in cars and clothes. Through it all, she balanced bills and kept her appearance so that he was proud of her.

"Our marriage is finished. I won't overlook this new affair. He claimed this young widow needed help with her taxes! He slept with her!" Connie's voice was flat and brittle.

"What about Buddy?" Her grandson was so quiet, always snacking—getting heavy.

"Stew doesn't see him. He never attends a soccer practice, or a school program. He'll see him more often when the judge sets visitation times." Connie sounded bitter. "Don't think badly of me. I tried. I really tried."

Kitt hugged Connie again and murmured, "Dad and I will be here for you." She knew it was a hollow answer. She wished she were far away. She didn't want the strain of conflict—a future of tears—an angry daughter—a confused grandson—an ex son-in-law. She drove home, drained. Her own face might even change like her mother's did after an operation for skin cancer. People turned away from looking at her mother's scarred skin. Life was unfair. Connie knew that she had worked very hard so that awful things could not disturb her life or her perfect face.

When Leon came home from work, he asked about her lunch with Connie.

"Connie couldn't keep our date . . . something about Buddy's Cub Scout meeting," she lied.

Leon kissed her lightly. "Well, I'll take my best girl out for dinner."

"Fine," Kitt smiled. Later she would tell him about Connie and Stewart's impending divorce.

She looked in the mirror and saw two faint lines across her brow. Connie's announcement had already taken a toll. Tomorrow she'd make an appointment for a few pin-prick injections to smooth away lines. There was no need to look middle-aged in a time of crisis.

NOBODY ASKED BUDDY

My name is Buddy. I am nine years old.

One day my Dad came home from work. He said, "Buddy, ride your bike over to Zack's house and play with him."

"Stay at least an hour," Mom added with a frown.

Nobody asked me if I wanted to play with Zack.

I didn't play with Zack. Instead, I biked to the Sugar Maple on Pioneer Drive. I sat on the big roots a long time. I tried to figure out things. My Mom and Dad never smiled at each other anymore. They didn't sit close to each other on the sofa. They never laughed together either. Lots of time Mom and I ate alone and watched TV. Something wasn't right.

When I returned, Dad and Mom put me on the sofa between them.

"We both love you," Dad began, "but your Mom and I have decided not to live together anymore. You will still live here in the house with your Mom. I will move to an apartment. You can come and stay with me overnight."

So Dad moved to an apartment in Windsor Manor. Every other weekend he took me somewhere. We went either to the park or the aquarium or the zoo or the museum. I got tired of walking.

One day Dad hugged me tight. He said, "I want you to meet a special lady. She has two kids, Taylor and Tyler. You will like to play with them. Their Mom Ginger and I really like each other."

I said, "I want you to come home."

Dad looked angry. He said in a hard voice, "I can't do that. Taylor and Tyler will be your new friends. You must play with them."

Nobody asked me if I wanted to play with a couple of little kids.

One morning at breakfast, Mom said, "I need to work. I found a job at the courthouse. I will use a computer in a big office. I've found an apartment in Country Gardens We will live on the second floor."

"I won't see Zack anymore," I said. I poured orange juice in my glass until it spilled on the floor.

Mom yelled, "Stop that! Don't be difficult. Zack will still be your friend. You can make some new friends, too." She cried as she wiped up the spill.

I didn't drink my juice.

So we moved to an old three-story brick building. Our apartment was at the end of a long hall with lots of doors. Soon our door had black marks at the bottom because every time Mom unlocked it, the door stuck and she kicked it with her shoe.

Nobody asked me if I wanted to live on a second floor at the end of a long hall behind a door with black marks. Nobody.

Mom enrolled me in a new school. At recess I followed other kids to the playground. A big red-haired kid came up to me.

"What's your name?" he asked.

"Buddy."

"That's a little kid's name," he sneered. "What's your real name?"

"Stewart . . . like my Dad."

"That's a dumb name, too."

"He doesn't live with us anymore," I added.

"Mine, neither."

I followed him to the ball diamond and stood behind the fence. The red-haired kid was the catcher. Nobody asked me to play ball.

One night when Mom came home, she pointed to the garbage bag. "Please, Buddy, take the garbage downstairs."

I held my nose. "Yuk! I don't like trash bins. They smell yucky."

Mom got cross. "I'm too tired to take it down tonight."

"I'm tired, too . . . too tired to climb back up the stairs."

"Don't argue!" Mom snapped. "Just do it! You're the man of the house now."

Then she began to cry. So I took the garbage downstairs. I never asked to be the man of the house.

Mom came home from work one night. She was all smiles and hummed a little tune. "We're having a guest tonight," she said and fixed caramelized onions and carrots. Then she put a meat loaf from the deli in the oven and tossed a salad.

I hated that carrot dish, but I didn't say anything because I liked to see Mom smile.

"Is Dad coming back?" I asked.

"No!" she snapped. "Don't ever ask that question again!" Her voice got lighter. "Our guest is a man named Floyd. He's a policeman. His wife died of cancer three years ago. I met him through a friend at work."

I wondered if Floyd carried a gun. The buzzer rang and Mom told me to answer the door. Floyd stood there, tall and smiling. His blue eyes crinkled at the corners when he grinned. His gray hair was short and wavy on top. His hands were big. He shoved his right hand at me.

"Good evening," he said with a booming voice. "You must be Buddy. Your Mom told me about you."

I didn't shake his hand. I looked down at his shoes. They

were very shiny, but one had a broken lace knotted together.

Mom pushed me forward and ordered, "Buddy, shake hands."

I shook his big paw. I didn't look at him. Nobody asked me if I wanted to meet Floyd.

Every other week-end when I was with Mom, Floyd took us somewhere—to the park or to the aquarium or to the zoo or to the museum (which I had seen the week before with my Dad and Ginger's two smart-alecky kids). I got tired of walking. Everyone thought I had a good time.

One Saturday afternoon, Mom said, "Instead of going somewhere, Floyd will bring his daughter to dinner tonight. She goes to college in California. Her name is Kelly."

That night this Kelly-person came to meet us. She looked at me and I looked at her.

She asked, "Once I played a clarinet in the school band. Do you play anything?"

"I play dominoes," I said.

Everyone thought it was funny.

I said, "I mean I just play games," .

Kelly was nice. She said, "Let's play dominoes after dinner."

We did, and I won two games.

Several months went by and Floyd hung around a lot. One night, I sat between him and Mom.

"Your Mom and I want to get married soon," Floyd said. "Then you can live in my house."

Mom looked happy. "It will be nice to live in a house again. Don't you think so, Buddy?"

"I dunno." I shrugged my shoulders.

I liked living alone with Mom. Dad lived in Ginger's house. I was never alone with him. Now I would never be alone with Mom anymore.

On a Saturday morning, I went to the courthouse with Mom. Kelly came with Floyd. She wore a green dress. Mom had a new yellow dress. I had a new yellow shirt with a blue tie. Yuk!

The Judge asked Mom, "Will you have this man for your husband?"

Mom smiled at Floyd and said, "Yes."

Then the Judge asked Floyd if he wanted Mom for a wife.

Nobody asked me if they should get married.

We moved into Floyd's house. There was an old swing set in the back yard. He said we could give it a new coat of paint. I said I was too old to play on a swing. I wanted to see his guns. He said he kept his guns at the Police station, but he could find me a badge if I wanted one. I said, "Skip it!"

Mom showed me my new room. It had brown carpet and some new brown and gold drapes.

Mom gave me a little push. "Tell Floyd that you like the new drapes."

"I like the new drapes."

Floyd gave me a long look. "This place is new to you and a little strange. This has been like an empty house with Kelly away at college. It's good to have you here."

He didn't seem too bad. He had a dog Rusty who licked my hand right away.

Floyd smiled at me. "I'm not your Dad, but we can be friends. Some people don't like policemen, so I need a lot of friends. I need you for a friend."

I thought about what he said. As long as he didn't try to be my Dad, we could be friends. "Okay, we can be friends," I repeated, "if Rusty can sleep in my room."

Floyd nodded, "Sure," and Mom smiled some more.

So that's the way it is. I live in Floyd's house. Every other Wednesday, I go to Ginger's house for dinner. Then I stay there on alternate week-ends. She always complains about extra work.

It's the same with holidays. At Christmas, I spend Christmas Eve at Ginger's place and see Dad. Then I come back at midnight and spend Christmas Day with Mom and Floyd.

I get a lot of presents, but nobody asks me what I want.

I want to live in our old house with Mom and Dad.

FRENCH—THE LANGUAGE OF LOVE

When he came home from work, Henry smelled pot roast. No one–not even the finest New York restaurant–could match Irma's succulent dish. The meat would be a rich brown surrounded by glazed carrots and onions with properly roasted potatoes. Perfect.

Usually, Monday night meant leftovers from Sunday dinner. However, their week-end had been different. On Saturday, they attended a wedding because they knew the groom's parents. The soloist sang in a breathy voice. One bridesmaid kept tugging at her black strapless gown. The wedding dinner was worse with stringy chicken and a deejay who blasted the dancers with rock music. Terrible. He couldn't wait to leave.

After Sunday services, a brunch honored the church organist who was retiring. Henry thought *About time! We've had at least twenty-years of recycled postludes. Her favorite was fast and loud like an exclamation point.* Irma provided her ham-and-potato casserole for the serving table and not a bit was left. Irma's dishes were always a hit.

Yes, Henry thought, *we'll have a nice quiet evening. I'll read McCullough's latest biography and Irma can edit her garden newsletter. Life is good.*

However, when Irma greeted him, he knew this meal would be different. As she kissed him, he saw her sparkly earrings. She wore a long velvet skirt, usually reserved for holiday parties. Her white satin blouse had a wide lace collar. He noticed the kitchen table was bare except for an odd-looking apple thing. A new dessert?

"What's up?" Henry asked warily.

Irma gave him a broad smile. "We're eating in the dining room tonight."

"I guessed that. Just the two of us?

"We're in a rut . . . always eating at the kitchen table."

"I like a rut," Henry grunted. "I get enough surprises at work." Like the rumor that the company was for sale, but I won't worry Irma with that one.

Henry stared at the dining table. It was set with the antique Limoges china that Irma had inherited from her aunt. A low arrangement of pink carnations was flanked by pink tapers in silver holders. Both place settings included sterling silverware and their crystal wedding goblets. Everything was from so long ago, only used for special occasions. Now Henry was edgy. This wasn't a typical Monday night.

Irma handed him a bottle of champagne. "You may open it, Mon-sewer." She said *Monsieur* with a slight giggle. "I'll serve our plates."

Had he missed an anniversary? A birthday? Nothing came to mind as he popped the cork. He noticed a brochure and a small notepad by Irma's place filled with scribbles. He wasn't wearing his glasses so the words blurred.

Carefully, Henry asked, "What's the occasion?"

"I've a surprise! I won't tell until we eat." Irma sounded girlish, like a teenager on Prom night. Last fall, she wanted him to join a bridge tournament. He refused. He hoped she wouldn't bring that up again.

Henry placed a crisply ironed pink napkin in his lap and waited. Irma came in, bearing two plates—beautifully arranged servings of pot roast and vegetables with added green beans and a sprig of rosemary.

"I guessed the pot roast," he said, "and the green beans are a nice touch." She was up to something and he braced himself for the unexpected.

"Oh, these aren't any green beans," Irma replied, looking closely at her note-pad, "these are harry-cots ver-tee!" She flashed a triumphant smile and pointed to the potatoes. "These are pom-mees de ter-ree."

Henry suppressed any laughter. Even after all these years, he remembered the endless word drills in his high school French class. He'd been a diligent student because he dreamed of being a history professor. French was the language of diplomacy. The Korean War had changed everything. He became an accountant so he could sit at a desk to accommodate his wounded hip. With effort he buried any memory about shrapnel on a cold hill. When he returned from Korea, he met and married Irma. Two years later Edward was born. His son had died in that accident at the pioneer maple. He must not think about anything sad now. Concentrate on Irma.

Henry lifted his champagne glass. "Here's to vous!" He touched her glass with a slight ping.

Irma giggled with pleasure. "We're eating French tonight. Sort of—I got a French cook-book at the library."

"The beans aren't French-cut," he teased, but Irma missed it.

"This brochure came today. Dorrie mailed it to us."

"Dorrie . . .who?"

"Your cousin, Dorrie."

"No! I don't want to hear about her." Henry grimaced.

Dorrie was not his relative. Years ago, she and Harold briefly lived near them. Dorrie was into genealogy. She called everyone in the phone book with her maiden surname. She was so persistent that she looked for similar forms—Snyder, Schneider, Sneider, or Snider. She was sure that any and all were related to her. Irma was fascinated by Dorrie's charts. The two became friends. After Harold was transferred to Minneapolis, Dorrie and Irma still sent Christmas cards, although they'd never seen each other again.

Henry continued, "We've been over this before. Dorrie was never my cousin. She is not my cousin . . . nor will she ever be my cousin."

Irma didn't agree. "She might be your cousin. You both come from German stock in Pennsylvania."

"You forget. Dorrie's ancestors were from Lancaster. My great-grandfather was an orphan. His parents died in a diptheria epidemic. A peddler took him to Ligonier. That's west—clear across the state. He was raised by a German clergyman and his wife. That's where he got his German name." He added, "He could have been Irish, Finnish or Hungarian! No one knows!"

Irma stiffened, "You don't know. Maybe the minister and his wife were cousins of his parents. He could have been born a Schneider. Just because something can't be proved, doesn't mean it can't be true."

"What does our discussion have to do with pot-roast and green beans?" Henry added, a bit sarcastic. "Let me guess. Dorrie found our missing link. It's a bald-headed monkey. I've got his genes."

Irma raised her eyebrows. "Better than that! You're royalty!"

Henry laid down his fork. "I object. I intend to remain a middle-class American!"

"Dorrie found that you're related to King Henry of Navarre! You've even got his name!"

"King Henry had a queen and three mistresses. He's related to half of France." Henry muttered. "Until today, I was Dorrie's German cousin. Now, I'm supposed to be a Frenchman. Maybe I'm an illegal alien."

"Dorrie told me all about your ancestry this morning. I called her after this travel folder came." Irma handed Henry a three-fold glossy brochure, *An Ancestral Tour to Remember*—the title in bold italic letters flanked by gold fleur-de-lis.

Henry sobered. This was more than a December Christmas card. He glanced inside, which showed a twelve-day itinerary of France. Three days in Paris and the rest around the countryside, led by Dorrie and Harold. Of course.

Henry groaned. "Is this another scheme of Dorrie's? Like the clean-up of Indian Creek? She was almost sued by environmentalists for disturbing the duck nests."

Irma ignored his remark. "Harold has retired. Dorrie researched and found that one branch of your family came from Alsace-Lorraine. It passed between France and Germany in different wars. Anyway, King Henry is related in there somewhere . . . so that makes you practically royalty." She thought a moment. "In fact, Dorrie says that you should spell and pronounce your name the French way—with an i . . . On-ree."

"Irma, don't get involved with Dorrie's crazy schemes! Remember all those plastic ware parties? She conned you into giving too many of those. Wasn't she into baskets, too?"

Irma ignored his question. "I know the royalty-bit is crazy, but it sounds fun." Irma grew serious. "The point is . . . she and Harold have organized this tour. I think we ought to go."

"No way! Too many pickpockets."

"I've always wanted to see the Eiffel Tower at night," Irma said dreamily.

"Heights make you dizzy."

She touched his arm. "Just think—we could stroll along in the Luxembourg Gardens."

"Your feet will hurt. At least, mine will."

"We can cruise down the Seine. A view from a river is always different. We could go at night when the city is lit up."

"Rivers smell."

"Oh Henry, it will be so wonderful. . . like a second honeymoon."

"With forty other people along? Hardly?" He winced when he saw the price. "Do you see what this costs? Several thousand. It's expensive!"

"Dorrie says it's deluxe all the way. Best hotels. Best food. Best tour buses."

"Of course! Dorrie and Harold get their way paid and a cut from each traveler. No wonder they've planned a ritzy trip." He flipped over the brochure. "The optional trips to Giverny and Chartres are extra. Plus air fare. We might have to stay overnight in New York. It's foolish to spend our hard-earned money like that!"

"I don't think so. Other people travel."

"They're in debt, too. I'm an accountant, I know." Sternly, he said, "No way will we spend this kind of money. You forget the Depression. My parents taught me to save for a rainy day."

"You always say that!" Irma snapped. "I've saved for decades, waiting for that day. Well, let me tell you . . . when it comes, I hope it's a cloudburst! I'm gonna take our money and throw it all up in the air and let it wash down the gutters. Because that's what we save for—A RAINY DAY!" She stood up. "I'm finished. I'll bring your dessert. I don't want any." She grabbed the brochure and tossed it in the wastebasket.

Henry was numb. Irma was always so understanding, so able to accept his rational point of view. He didn't know how to respond to her anger. When she brought the dessert, he noticed it was on a kitchen plate.

"Here! It's an apple ta-teen or ta-tine or something like that."

"I'll help you with the dishes," Henry offered quietly.

"No! I'll wash the Limoges alone. Go read the paper when you're done with dessert."

That was what Henry tried to do. Except neither the paper nor the biography nor even Larry King's interview could replace his uneasiness over Irma's outburst.

Irma stood in the doorway. Henry noted that her eyes were red. She must have cried. She wore navy slacks and a faded sweatshirt with red roses across the front. "I want to finish the Wildflower page tonight. The club's newsletter must be mailed tomorrow."

"Irma, I'm sorry," Henry began, "that it's so much money . . ."

She cut him off. "It's okay. A trip's no fun if we don't agree. Anyway, your hip might hurt with all that riding. Go to bed when you're ready. I'll work late." She went down to the basement where she had her computer, desk and filing cabinet.

When Henry went to bed, he couldn't sleep. Irma crawled in beside him much later.

Irma was asleep when Henry left for work the next morning. He retrieved the travel folder and studied it at his desk with his daily coffee. He worked automatically as he checked reports and figures marched in columns before him.

Brandi, a new intern, came to his desk with a sheaf of print-outs. She stood there with her limp dyed-blonde hair. A wisp fell down one cheek. Her eyes were ringed with black mascara while her cheeks were powdered white and her lips were plum. She looked like a waif.

"I don't understand these," she shrugged, shoving the papers at him.

Henry was not surprised. In fact nothing surprised him with Brandi. In her first three weeks, Brandi (whose name was really Brenda, but she insisted on Brandi with an i) was frequently confused. Henry checked her papers while Brandi studied her blue fingernails. Suddenly, she reached across his desk and grabbed the travel brochure.

"Oh, France! How exciting!" she gushed. "Are you going? I just loved Paris."

Henry frowned. The girl must be mistaken. What would she know about France? She had been hired from some welfare-training program. She had a small daughter in the company day-care center and no husband.

"The folder was sent to my wife." Henry didn't want to waste company time with Brandi, but he was curious. "What do you know about Paris?"

Brandi grinned–more alert than at any time since she'd been hired. "I was there with kids from the West-Side Teen Club. Fourteen of us got to go. We did car-washes and stuff like that. Got a big grant from some foundation. The trip was to enrich us. Got our way paid and a hundred dollars for spending money. Paris was a blast!"

Henry was stunned. Brandi was barely twenty and had gone to France. Here he was, almost retired, and the closest he'd been was a trip to Montreal organized by the Lions Club.

He hesitated, afraid to ask. "And just what made Paris a blast?"

"We ate big Macs on the main drag."

"You mean the Champs Elysees?"

"Yeah, something like that. The burger tasted so-o-o good, after all that stuff with sauces. I mean French food is really stra—ange."

Henry stared at Brandi. How could anyone even think of a hamburger in Paris? "You saw Versailles? The Louvre?"

"Yeah, I guess. Everyplace was crowded." She brightened, "We found a really neat place for Texas chili. When you go, you really want to eat there. I got a T-shirt and long dangly earrings."

Henry turned to Brandi's sheets. He found only three mistakes, an improvement over last week's ten errors. He circled the wrong numbers and sent her back to her computer. Then he studied the travel brochure. How could anyone miss the thrill of historical sites?

When Henry took his afternoon coffee-break, Rosemary from Purchasing stopped him. "I hear you're going to Paris this summer. That's wonderful!" she smiled.

"Where'd you hear that?"

"Everyone knows in our department. You know how fast news travels around here."

Henry knew. Brandi had blabbed their conversation. That girl was even more irritating than before. People might assume that he and Irma could afford expensive vacations.

"Well, we haven't made a decision yet," Henry wavered.

Rosemary stirred her coffee. "Go while you can. My parents planned a trip down the Nile. Dad died from a heart-attack three days after his retirement party. Mom is still bitter that he'd never go anywhere."

As Henry left at five, Dorothea who was an Executive Assistant—which meant she was the personal secretary to a senior vice-president—walked to the parking lot with him. Dorothea was a gray-haired sensible woman.

"When do you leave for France?" Dorothea asked.

"So that rumor has reached the executive suite?"

"I'm so pleased for you. I told the others that you've always been so interested in history. Your conversations with Irma must be so stimulating. I envy her."

Henry hedged. "Irma and I haven't set any date. We're still thinking about it."

"Irma's so lucky to have you for a husband with your interest in travel. My ex was a real stick-in-the-mud. It was a relief when we divorced. Twenty-three years of boredom. Such a dull man." She climbed into the car and waved good-bye.

Henry still mulled over Dorothea's remark as he finished Irma's lemon soufflé dessert that night. Henry asked, "Am I dull? I mean . . . do you find living with me rather dull?" He sat at the kitchen table, shoulders slumped, as if awaiting a sentence.

Irma whirled around and stood behind his chair. She reached around his neck and nuzzled his shoulder.

"Dull? Not my Henry!" she said. "You may be quiet, a bit reserved. But that's much different from being dull. Why, you're the best-read person I know. I remember how proud Edward was. He told the other kids that you were the smartest Dad in the whole world!" She sounded like a lawyer before a jury. "My mother always said, *Still water runs deep.* That's the way you are. Other men spout off about sports or taxes. You know more than any of them, but you don't brag or put them down. You KNOW things. You LISTEN. You never make anyone look foolish." She gave him a quick hug. "I wouldn't have you any other way."

Henry went to the den and thought about Irma. She was loving and loyal. She had supported him as he recovered from his Korean War wounds. Both had absorbed the shock and quietly grieved over Edward's death. They lived simply and found solace through the rhythm of work, Irma's garden, worship on Sunday and their annual vacation at a fishing resort on Sand Lake. Irma would never admit it, but Henry knew—he was a dull person.

Maybe it was time to take a big trip—one they could remember. If a tour guide impressed the tourists with elaborate stories, he'd give Irma the right facts back in their hotel room. Yes, he'd sneak Irma away from Dorrie and Harold for a private tete-a-tete at some small café—a time they could always recall on a cold winter night. Irma would remember the trip even when she was widowed. Dear God, I don't want Irma to be bitter. Not that.

Henry was in such a hurry the next morning that he forgot his brown bag lunch. At noon, he refused to join the others at a new Chinese restaurant. Instead he hurried off to the huge book store several blocks away.

When he reached the Travel section, he took his time. He wanted the right book about France. He chose one with lots of colored pictures, a thumbnail history and good index. Then he found a purse-size French/English phrase book—not that Irma would ever pronounce anything correctly. She wouldn't need it with their English speaking guides, but she'd have fun. He'd help her pronounce French words, too. He chose a Monet-print wrapping paper and asked the clerk to tie his package with lavender moiré ribbon.

First, he wrote on the travel flyleaf, "Please, take me to Paris, too. Je t'aime. Henri."

BREAKFAST MEETING

When he heard his ex-wife's voice on the phone, Stewie braced himself. Years ago when they were married, he thought of Connie as a piece of peppermint candy—sweet and pink and pretty. Since their divorce eight years ago, she'd become more like peanut brittle—hard, unyielding and just as nutty. Her voice fairly crackled.

"Look, would I bother you if this wasn't important?" she said. "I know you're so terribly busy . . . " jabbing the needle a little harder, " . . . but I'm terribly worried about Buddy. I'm really terribly worried," she repeated.

Stewie knew from Connie's tone that this was serious. Buddy was their son, almost seventeen. He was named Stewart, Junior, but he'd been nicknamed Buddy by Connie's Dad and the name stuck.

Stewie tried to remember if his child-support check was overdue. He ran his hand through graying hair and realized how thin it was on top. Even though he worked out at the gym twice a week, his waistline seemed to sag. Why did he always seem middle-aged and weary after a strained conversation with Connie? She could really make him feel miserable.

Connie rushed on. "I found a small envelope in his backpack last night. It might be Ecstasy. Drugs are in the high school now."

That was like Connie. She exaggerated things. When they were married, Connie questioned him if he came home late. She was angry when she found out that he and Ginger lunched together. An office flirtation meant nothing. Women must be like that. Now Ginger ragged him about him about giving Samatha, a young Public Relations intern, an occasional ride home after work.

"Are you listening?" Connie snapped.

Stewie mumbled, "Sure. Did you ask him about drugs?" He knew there were drugs in school, but Buddy had no reason to get involved. The kid had everything—a new computer, electronic games, a cell phone. Maybe next year, a car. What else did he need?

"He denied it, of course, but I'm not sure. I thought if you just talked to him."

Stewie sighed. It wasn't only work, but arranging a meeting with Buddy that was difficult. Before their marriage, Ginger called Buddy a cutie—like a teddy bear. After they married and Lance was born (a name that Ginger chose, but Stewie didn't like), Ginger became upset when he had any contact with Buddy.

Ginger complained, "Buddy's a big boy. He has his own life. He doesn't need to lean on you."

It had been almost two months since he'd seen his older son. Stewie looked at his schedule. "Maybe I can arrange something next week."

Connie sounded scared. "See him right away! It's been awhile. Set up something for tomorrow . . . before or after school. He needs to hear from YOU . . . to know you're concerned, too. He promised to go straight home after school, but how do I know? I get caught in evening traffic."

Connie worked in the courthouse downtown. She was remarried to a policeman named Floyd. Recently, they moved to a townhouse. Floyd had a grown daughter somewhere out west—Arizona or California. Floyd should know about kids and drugs. Stewie thought, *Floyd ought to give Connie some help.*

Usually when Connie called, she wanted more money.

Last month Stewie had sent an extra check for Buddy's new room. Ginger got mad and clammed up—gave him a cold shoulder for a week. Things went better after he took Ginger and the kids to a downtown hotel for a swim week-end. Ginger's kids ate a lot of free popcorn and ordered pizza for breakfast. They smelled like chlorine for two days. It was noisy and cramped. If it weren't for Lance, Stewie thought, he might walk away. No, he must never consider that as long as Lance was young. Just think about Buddy now.

"Okay. Okay," Stewie answered. "I'll call Buddy and set up something."

Connie hung up without a word. Stewie sat at his desk, stringing paper clips until he worked out his plan. He would meet Buddy tomorrow morning for an early breakfast before school. If he used the office phone, his cell phone statement wouldn't have Buddy's number on it. Ginger would never know. He'd make an excuse to Ginger that he had an early meeting. Probably she wouldn't find out about breakfast with Buddy. He'd meet his son at the shopping mall close to the high school. It would be good to see Buddy again.

That night Stewie congratulated himself that all had gone smoothly. Ginger was in high spirits because her two kids brought home good report cards. Five-year-old Lance knew most of his alphabet. Stewie took them out to dinner at a family buffet place, just in case Ginger found out about his breakfast plan. He could argue that he treated all the kids the same way.

When he parked the next morning, Stewie saw Buddy leaning against a mall window. He caught his breath, because in the last two months Buddy seemed even larger. His son not only looked taller, but plump and hefty—a beefy kid in baggy black pants and an old Packers' green-and-gold sweatshirt. Stewie wondered if it was one he'd thrown away when the divorce happened years ago. Buddy's blonde hair was pink. Maybe the kid had a tattoo somewhere. He really didn't know much about Buddy anymore.

Stewie hugged his son, and they walked through the mall together, making stabs at conversation.

"It's great to get together." Stewie began "Sorry it's so early . . . hope it won't make you late to class."

Buddy shrugged, "Who cares? I've study hall the first hour."

There was a dollar-ninety-nine special with eggs, sausage, fried potatoes and toast. Stewie ordered the eggs scrambled and coffee. Buddy fidgeted and asked for a skillet meal—which was the same order except it cost two dollars more in a fry pan plus a root beer. Stewie winced. Root beer with eggs? Kids were hard to understand.

They faced each other. Buddy hunched over the table and wolfed down huge bites, scarcely looking up. His silence and his hurried meal left Stewie uncomfortable. Connie ought to teach Buddy some manners—at least to sit up straight. Meeting this way wasn't so easy after all.

Stewie tried a question. "Is school okay?"

Buddy nodded.

"How about your teachers . . . any really good ones? How about classes?"

Buddy wrinkled his nose. "All okay."

Only the scraping of chairs by other diners filled the silence between them.

"How about activities?" Stewie probed. "You should try out for football."

Buddy pushed aside his empty skillet. "It's for jocks." He bit his thumbnail, "You always ask the same questions . . . classes, teachers, sports. I tell you nothing's new. Nothing!"

Stewie took a deep breath. "I hear there's a lot of drugs, like Ecstasy, around school."

"You gonna get on my case?" Buddy flared. His eyes squinted hard, so that his cheeks puffed out even more on his moon face. He emptied his root beer glass.

Stewie looked straight at him. "I'm concerned. We're all concerned."

"Don't give me that! You don't worry about me! You've got another family!"

Did Connie feed Buddy that line? Stewie continued smoothly. "Your Mom called and we talked. We both want the best for you."

Buddy gave him a wary look. "So . . . that's why you walked away from us?"

Stewie shifted in his seat. Somehow the tables were turned. Now Buddy asked the questions.

"I didn't walk away. It's just that . . . that your Mom and I didn't agree about things anymore. It had nothing to do with you. We both loved . . . love you."

"Yeah, I know, but not enough to work things out." Buddy stood up. "Look, I gotta go to school."

" . . . But I thought we could talk awhile."

Buddy remained standing. "What's there to talk about? You live in Ginger's house. Mom lives in a townhouse with Floyd . . . the guy with a badge!" He gave a cynical grunt. "Huh! He thinks he knows everything!"

Stewie began to argue. "You've got a nice room. Your Mom told me how she fixed up the basement in their new condo for you. I paid for your desk." Silence. Stewie added, "You can always come to our place for the week-end."

Stewie knew this wasn't true. When Buddy slept in the basement playroom, Ginger complained that he took up too much room. She said that her kids needed the space. Even though Buddy was Connie's problem, Ginger needed to lighten up, too. However, he wouldn't dare argue with his second wife.

Buddy stood up and adjusted his backpack. He stiffened and stared hard at Stewie. "Tell me where do I belong?"

Stewie was flustered. "With both of us . . . your Mom and me. You've got two homes."

"Bull! You sound like a high school counselor. The point is—I have no home. So don't waste your time! Don't tell me what to do!" Buddy turned and walked quickly away without looking back.

Stunned, Stewie sat there and watched Buddy disappear down an escalator. Somehow his son was riding out his life. Stewie pushed away his own half-finished plate. The home fries looked greasy and the scrambled eggs were cold. Even his coffee tasted bitter.

He wanted to run after Buddy—hold him—tell him it was all a mistake. Buddy was a good kid—he had to be. After all, Buddy was his son.

Stewie was sure that he loved Buddy. He wanted the kid to have a home. Stewie knew he couldn't promise that—or anything. Something had gone wrong—terribly wrong—for both of them.

HENRY'S SILENT WAR

More than anything else, Henry wanted peace and quiet. He had enough of keyboard clatter and office chatter at Holton and Saunders. He liked to recline in his big brown lounge chair, ease his hip, read a little and doze. His day at work had been stressful. Pain from his old shrapnel injury from the Korean War returned. He took pain pills on his morning coffee break. Then the computers went down for an hour after lunch. Mid-afternoon, he heard another rumor that the firm was for sale. It had not been a good day.

What will happen to me? He knew. He would retire. He'd been hired by old Saunders after the Korean War. Now Saunders was dead, and Holton had been gone even longer. Retirement would please Irma. She wanted to winter in Florida and travel. Henry knew his own days would be empty. He couldn't golf, and staying in a strange place without his lounge chair would be even less enjoyable. So what was left? Empty days—empty time.

Memories were left—memories that he didn't want to relive. Once there had been many flashbacks. He had overcome those with Irma's help. If he had time on his hands, would he think about the past? Think about Eddie's death? No, he didn't want that.

When the phone rang, Irma answered. "Well, I suppose he could," she said slowly. "He has a box of things—his uniform, discharge papers, clippings—things like that—down in the basement." She clapped her hand over the mouthpiece, "It's Ginger. Her stepson Buddy needs to interview a veteran for a history report. She thought of you."

Henry shook his head. Certainly Irma knew he never talked about Korea to anyone–even to her. "It was too long ago. Tell Ginger to find someone else.

He picked up The Times in the den. His hands shook as he tried to read the headlines. The whole world was going crazy, including his own.

Irma followed him. "I can't turn Ginger down. You know how touchy she is. If you don't help Buddy, it's like you've turned her down, too. There's enough trouble between Ginger and Buddy. Maybe this will help both of them."

Henry wondered if anything could help Ginger. What was her relationship to them anyway? Eddie died and she remarried. Did that make her an ex? She was the mother of Taylor and Tyler, their only grandchildren. And where had she found those names? Ginger and the grandchildren were in-and-out of their lives like wild canaries.

Henry scowled. "I don't talk abut Korea. I never joined the Legion. I don't march in parades. I don't need to answer questions from some kid who's waited until the last minute to do his assignment." The kid might be like his young co-workers who were sloppy and careless. Henry knew he didn't understand young people. "Korea was a postscript to World War II. Nobody cares about it."

"That's not true," Irma argued. "Maybe you should talk about it even at this late date."

"I can't and I won't! Korea is a forgotten war . . . an early Viet-Nam." He turned up the volume so Irma would stop talking.

She turned it down and said flatly. "Buddy will be here at seven. I invited him. Be polite. Answer questions. He won't ask many. Ginger says he's a quiet kid."

"If the kid's found a way to avoid Ginger, he must be smart!"

Irma shook her head and left the room. He tried to

forget—to erase the memory of Korea. He liked being an accountant because he could lose himself in numbers and not think about the past. No kid was going to open up old wounds. If Irma invited him, she could talk—except she didn't know anything.

After the war, he'd passed his CPA exams and started working. He met Irma at a bus stop. They stood in silence for two months. One morning she shyly asked about the Lincoln biography he carried. They traded books two weeks later. It began a friendship that eventually led to marriage. She was the only girl he'd ever dated. With her encouragement, they married and had a real home—even a son, Eddie. She made his recovery possible.

Henry loved Irma–even her offbeat remarks. People liked her, so he was invited places even though he knew people found him self-contained. They didn't know his terrible secret.

Henry was surprised at Buddy's appearance. The kid looked awful with ill-fitting black pants and a sweat-shirt with a rock star logo. His tennis shoes were bulky and out-sized, half-tied across the instep. Henry wanted to warn him about stumbling on his ties, but the kid might resent it. Sloppy—the kid was plain sloppy. Where was his mother? He watched Buddy open a green-spiral notebook and nervously fiddle with a pencil.

"Where'd you serve?" Buddy asked, hunched over–his body too big for Irma's Queen Anne chair. "I mean–were you an officer?"

Henry relaxed. The interview would soon be over. Buddy didn't want to be there either. Henry said he joined the Marine Reserves to get a small stipend so he could go to Business school. Then Korean fighting began, and the Marines were called up unexpectedly. Henry grimly remembered the surprise that his company felt because the

Army was in Korea to do the fighting. What did it matter to Buddy? Henry stretched his leg. He'd been hit with more than shrapnel. He would always carry his wounds.

Irma interrupted. "I'll bet Buddy would like to see your uniform . . . and the medals from Korea."

Henry wished Irma would go to the kitchen. Load the dishwasher or something. She liked to wipe fingerprints from the refrigerator.

Buddy's eyes widened. "You still got your uniform? Maybe I could borrow it."

"It wouldn't fit you. I haven't touched it in years."

"I'd like to see it. A recruiter comes to school. He looks real sharp."

"Oh, Henry will show it to you," Irma said proudly. "Henry was a real hero. He was hit by shrapnel. That's why he limps. Got a Purple Heart and everything."

Henry turned away. Irma would never understand. Lots of GI's got medals. Fifty-thousand killed in Korea. He was one of a hundred thousand wounded. There was nothing special about his medal. Just a reminder that he had been there . . . oh, how he had been there.

Irma pointed to the basement. "Go ahead. We'll have ice cream when you finish."

Henry clumped downstairs with Buddy behind him. He opened the trunk and there was his uniform, folded neatly in a plastic bag. He took it out and shook it a little. It had been years since he touched it. He never resisted going to Korea. Marines did their duty and fought for their country. He still felt an unspoken pride that he'd been a Marine.

Buddy fingered the brass buttons with a quick glance—like he couldn't believe that such an old man had once worn such a slim trim uniform.

"What about souvenirs? Like guns . . . or enemy daggers?" Buddy asked, ignoring the clippings. The kid had seen too many Kung-Fung—whatever they were named—

movies.

Henry hesitated. He had souvenirs, but not any he wanted to share. "Irma has a small floral screen upstairs. I sent that home to my Mom. And a couple of vases. Go on upstairs and have some ice cream," Henry pointed to the stairway. "I'll close this trunk. Be there shortly."

He heard Buddy and Irma's voices float down to him. Henry reached into the trunk and pulled out a small box. It held pictures that came back in his nightmares. Once he tried to throw the box away, but he couldn't. It proved the war was real—that he hadn't imagined the awful scenario. He handled each item quietly, thoughtfully—remembering.

His Marine regiment arrived in Korea, expecting to be there only a few weeks. General MacArthur promised to be home for Christmas. What did he know from his command post in Japan? Rumors spread that MacArthur's old maps were flawed. He was completely mistaken about the Chinese Communists. The General was so sure they'd never enter the war. Instead, the gooks came in hordes—three Chinese divisions against three Marine regiments. He and his buddies almost felt sorry for the gooks in their cotton jackets and thin tennis shoes.

Everyone suffered from the cold—bone-chilling cold. On the ridge his life changed forever. The Chinese were in bunkers and fox-holes. Their trench warfare seemed out of a World War I history book. The Marines had to take the ridge, so they climbed up the back mountainside—slowly inching up as snow fell. Slippery rocks. Sliding backwards. Toeholds in waist-deep snow. They grabbed at scrub bushes—anything to keep from falling. Impossible, but they finally made it, like ants crawling up a log barrier.

Over the top, they tossed grenades to capture the bunkers below. They found many gooks outside—already dead, frozen as if they were asleep on a snow blanket.

Henry picked up a faded picture of a small Oriental girl.

He'd taken if off a dead body when they cleared out the bunker. Supplies were scarce, and his buddies took anything they could. He found the child's picture. Somehow, he couldn't toss it away. He kept it with him.

During the day, there would be a peculiar stand-off. Neither side wanted to reveal its position. Shelling began at night. A gook might yell that his unit wanted to surrender. Or they would come out of a hut, dressed like peasants. It didn't matter where or when, Henry learned to spray the area with gunfire. Once he saw a baby fly out of a mother's arms. He felt his stomach churn and tried to forget it.

For five days, their platoons were surrounded. Radio contact was lost. He and Shorty started out on patrol. As they reached midway, they saw two figures loom above them. Gooks with grenades, they thought. They both fired. The bodies fell. When they reached them, the dead were Marines from the other platoon. Shorty went crazy until the sergeant knocked him out to silence him. Henry vomited and stumbled into the hospital tent for help. Instead, the medic pressed him to give morphine to the badly wounded.

Two weeks later when he was hit by shrapnel, he found it a kind of relief—as if somehow his mistake was being squared. However, memories of killing innocent peasants and his own buddies wouldn't go away.

He returned home with nightmares. His father didn't understand and berated him to get over it—act like a man. His mother cried a lot. Finally, he moved to an apartment and started at Holton and Saunders. Then he met Irma. She didn't ask questions—just held him tightly when he cried out in his sleep.

Henry sat on the bottom step, waiting for Buddy to leave. He should have told the kid about the war—done more for him. Just as he should have done more for Edward, his son. He was afraid to love Edward too much because he might lose him, another sacrifice for his mistakes in the war.

Edward died anyway.

When he married Irma, he started back to church. Through the years, he was Council treasurer, communed and found some solace in the liturgy especially the Benediction, *God bless and keep you and make his countenance shine upon you and give you peace.* Frequently, he reread his Catechism. As a boy, he'd memorized the Ten Commandments. He knew the Fifth by heart—*Thou shall not kill.* Along with Luther's explanation—*We should fear and love God that we may not hurt or harm our neighbor in his body, but help and befriend him in every bodily need.*

The Chaplain told Henry that his mistake was an accident of war, not deliberate murder. Still, Henry knew that he had killed his buddies.

Opening this trunk brought it all back. It didn't matter what others said, he had broken the Fifth Commandment. He had killed both the enemy and his comrades. Henry buried his head in his hands. Would he ever find peace?

ALONE TOGETHER

More than anything else, Buddy wanted to belong—to someplace or to someone. He stood under the Sugar Maple, feeling miserable and alone. His Mom and Floyd were in New Orleans. He had to stay at Ginger's place while they were gone. After his "huffing" night a month ago, neither parent trusted him. That was a stupid thing to do—trying to prove to the guys that he wasn't scared of doing drugs. Instead, he'd passed out. The other kids called 9-1-1 and scattered. He woke up in ER. Floyd and his Mom returned. His Dad didn't come that night, but met him for another breakfast several days later. Now his classmates avoided him, afraid that he'd rat on them. Instead of being accepted, he was more alone than before.

When he faced History class, he wasn't well prepared. That old veteran Henry didn't tell him much the night before. But then, what did he ask him? Buddy couldn't remember and didn't care. When the tardy bell rang, Buddy slumped down in his seat, hoping Mr. Burroughs would call on someone else. His classmates were divided in their opinions of their teacher. Under their breath they called him Mr. Boring. His best students, like that new girl Cheryl, found him fair but demanding. Buddy just wanted a passing grade.

Buddy knew he wasn't laid back, lazy or dumb, but boring Burroughs might think so. His oral report was on today's schedule. He knew his report was poor. He dreaded facing old Boring who was middle-aged with a white shirt, a red bow tie and wing-tipped shoes. Buddy just wanted out of school so he could get on with his life.

Buddy's paper shook in his sweaty hands. "I interviewed a Korean War veteran named Henry."

Mr. Burroughs interrupted. "Class, if you remember, three-fourths of your grade will be on historical research and interview material. One fourth will be on your oral report. Now, Buddy, straighten up and give us your report as if you were teaching this class."

Some girls giggled as Buddy stood taller. He noticed Cheryl gave him an encouraging smile. He cleared his throat and began again.

"Well, this Henry-person took me downstairs to an old trunk. When he opened it up, he showed me his uniform. It had a shoulder patch. He got a medal, a Purple Heart."

"Did you see it?"

"No."

"Why not?"

"He didn't want me to see it. His wife showed me a couple of souvenirs. The Korean War was a long time ago. Henry didn't want to talk about it. That's my report."

Buddy walked back to his seat and plopped down.

Mr. Burroughs jiggled his pencil before he marked his grade book. "Buddy, tell me, why was the United States involved in Korea? Where did this Henry-person fight? What does the thirty-eighth parallel have to do with the United States and Korea today?" He waited. "Give us some answers."

"I dunno," Buddy mumbled.

"Research was part of the assignment. You can go to the library, or log on to a computer . . . "

Buddy nodded and kept his eyes on the floor. What was the use of telling old Boring that he had to stay at Ginger's house while his Mom and Floyd were off somewhere? After school he baby-sat Lance while Ginger took Taylor to the dance studio and Tyler to karate lessons. Every afternoon they left—swimming or ice-skating or soccer games. Her kids were constantly climbing into the van and dashing off. Ginger said that Lance was an Attention Deficit Syndrome kid—difficult to take places. Silently, Buddy disagreed. If anything Lance suffered from Attention Needed Syndrome. Lance was a quiet kid when he played Parcheesi or Checkers with him. If he ever had a kid, he'd sure pay more attention than Ginger or his Dad did to Lance.

It was impossible to use a computer at Ginger's house. Taylor who was in Middle School and already a snob, grabbed the machine when she got home and would only share it with Tyler. Buddy waited until the three kids were in bed and started to log on the Internet. Then Ginger came into the den and said she needed it for e-mail and her chat-room friends. Buddy gave up any research and crawled into his sleeping bag downstairs next to Lance. He couldn't blurt out any of this to old Boring.

His teacher didn't cut him down in front of the class. "Well," said Mr. Burroughs, "perhaps there were reasons why this Henry-person didn't respond. I'll extend your time one more week if you do background research. Or you can take a D for your grade."

Buddy bit his lip. "My Mom won't be back for ten days. I gotta take care of my half-brother sometimes." Why try to explain? "I guess I'll take the grade."

"Let me know if you change your mind." Mr. Burroughs said. "Cheryl, you're next."

Buddy watched Cheryl, who sat two rows across from him, pull out a map. She had pictures plastered on poster board. She even had a small flag. Some relative in Vermont had faxed a diary and sent pictures of his crew who flew the Pacific in World War II. He'd even been on Tinian Island when the Enola Gay dropped the Atom Bomb.

It was obvious that the class was as impressed as Mr. Burroughs.

After class, Buddy sat on the sidelines in the cafeteria. His daily hamburger and French fries hung heavy in his stomach. He didn't listen to the crude remarks made by other guys. Suddenly, Buddy realized that Cheryl stood beside him.

"Look, Buddy," she said earnestly, "I know that Henry-person from church. He's really a quiet man. He doesn't mix with people during coffee hour. Hardly talks to anyone. If you need a computer for research, come home with me this afternoon." Cheryl offered. "I've got my own, and my Mom has one in the kitchen. You can use either one."

Some guy gave a low whistle. She snapped at him. "I just want to help. Why don't you get Buddy on-line so he can get a decent grade?" She turned on her heels and walked back to her table.

Another guy called over, "Wow! Did you see those brown eyes? And more?"

Buddy looked in her direction. He didn't see anything, but a friendly girl—a classmate who offered him help. He needed to pass History, if he were to graduate. He had to get his diploma, get out of school and get a job. Ginger always reminded him that his Dad's child-support payments would end when he was eighteen. His Mom casually hinted that after graduation, he should move to his own apartment. Where? How?

Buddy took a deep breath and walked over to Cheryl's table. "It's real good of you to offer some help with that Korean stuff. Can I really come over after school?"

"Meet me outside. My Mom's at a meeting this afternoon, so we'll have to walk home. I don't live too far. Okay?"

Buddy told Ginger that he couldn't baby-sit after school. She snapped that she'd tell his Dad that he was goofing off. Furthermore, since he was with them for two weeks now, it would count against his allotted time in summer. He hung up on her.

Buddy found that Cheryl was even nicer when she helped

him with his report. When he handed in his paper the next day, old Boring gave him a C-plus. At lunch, he sat at her table. It was easy to talk to her.

"If I graduate, I'll owe it to you." he grinned.

"School is rough sometimes. We moved here last fall. The other girls have their friends from grade school. It's hard to get acquainted," Cheryl sighed. "It's good to have one friend."

Buddy noticed the guys were right. She had beautiful brown eyes, like a fawn. Her long dark hair was curly with pink enamel clips that matched her blush pink lips. There was nothing flashy or cheap about Cheryl.

One morning a few guys waited while he went to his locker. When he opened it, a dozen packages of condoms fell out. Buddy turned red. The guys were laughing. One made a thumbs-up sign. Another winked. He slammed the locker hard. As he passed by, he heard a hiss, "When you gonna score?"

More than anything else, Cheryl wanted to go to the Senior Prom. When her parents moved to Whittimore last summer, she felt alone—like Buddy. Her senior year was dull. If she could go to the dance, at least she'd have one happy memory. Even before Christmas, other girls discussed Prom dresses and hair styles. She didn't own a formal. All she had was a fistful of report cards—even from elementary school—with an A in almost every subject.

Over Christmas vacation, she flew back to see her childhood friend Valerie. During their months apart, Valerie gained her first boyfriend. Cheryl felt she was unwanted when the three of them went to a movie. She missed having a special friend. If Buddy really liked her, she would write to Valerie that she had a boyfriend, too.

Cheryl knew her mother worked hard to make their new home pleasant. She hired a decorator for Cheryl's bedroom.

It looked strange with new French furniture, pale pink drapes and a muted green rug, just like a glossy magazine page. She hated it.

"I miss my old Cabbage Patch dolls and the Mickey Mouse poster from our first trip to Disney World," she complained moodily.

Her mother Myra replied, "Your new room is beautiful. It cost a small fortune. . . not that I'm complaining. Please, say *Thank-you* to your Dad with a smile."

Maybe throwing out favorite things went with her Dad's big promotion, but her own life wasn't necessarily better. Only lonely and boring. She was cut in volleyball tryouts. She ushered at the Valentine variety show. No one asked her to the cast party.

What did graduation even mean? She was accepted at the University, but why go? She had no friends there. If high school were this lonely, a big university would be worse. Maybe McNaughton College would be okay until she knew what she wanted to do. Right now, she needed a date for the Senior Prom. That would brighten the last two months of school.

When she offered help to Buddy that noon, Cheryl really felt sorry for him. Also, he might need a Prom date. Other kids teased him terribly, but he seemed a nice guy. He never hit anyone when he was called *Fatso*. He walked away with hunched shoulders, staring at the ground.

Cheryl knew hurt, too. An Honors student accused Cheryl that her relative had really prepared her history report when so much material was faxed to her.

"You just stood there and read his stuff," the student complained.

Buddy came to her defense. "Cheryl did her own research. I saw it. I was there."

"Thanks, Buddy. I need your support."

"The other kids are jealous. Anyway, you're prettier than

any other girl." He paused, "Thanks to you, I'll pass History. Will you be home after school? I'll drop by."

Buddy arrived, bringing her mother a small pot of yellow primroses.

Her mother was impressed. "Such a polite boy, but he looks a trifle scruffy."

"He's not scruffy!" Cheryl flared. "All the guys wear baggy pants. At least, he talks to me at lunch, which is more than the jocks do!" She slammed her bedroom door and fell across the flowered spread. It wasn't long until the Prom. She needed Buddy to ask her. Quickly!

Next morning, she found Buddy's locker and stood there. She asked if he needed to use her computer again after school. She shared her lunchtime sandwich with him. In turn, he invited her to the large building supply store where he worked on week-ends.

Cheryl borrowed her mother's car on Saturday and found Buddy amid electrical supplies, unloading boxes of floodlights. Proudly, he showed off fixtures. They were on an upper landing where there were few customers. It was like being alone in another world.

"We've got everything for a home," Buddy boasted, "If you need something like light bulbs, I can get them at a discount."

Carefully, Cheryl said, "Are you going to the Prom this year?"

Buddy shrugged his shoulders. "Me? I dunno. I don't dance very well."

Cheryl looked away. "I don't either, but it sounds like fun."

Buddy didn't answer.

Cheryl, desperate, said she'd pick him up after work. Maybe they could have a coke and talk about graduation.

That night Cheryl drove along Pioneer Drive. When they came to the great Sugar Maple, Buddy said, "Stop! This is where I always wait before going to Ginger's house. Or back to Floyd's place. I always figure things out here."

Cheryl parked nearby so they could watch the pale white moon above the maple. It was a soft spring night. A gentle breeze rustled the leaves to whisper encouragement to friends and lovers.

Buddy asked slowly, "Do you really want to go to the Prom?"

"Well . . . sure."

"Gee, I'll take you. I'll rent a suit, but I don't have money for a limo. Or a fancy dinner. Or stuff like that."

"We can use this car," Cheryl replied with shining eyes. "I don't care where we eat. Anyway, I don't like the noise in those big banquet rooms."

"I'm saving my money to get my own place after I graduate. We'll eat at the Grecian Gardens, if that's okay. They have Saturday night specials. Sometimes I eat there alone after work. They have big dinners, and then I don't have to eat Ginger's cooking."

Cheryl was impressed that Buddy would soon have his own apartment. "That means you won't have a curfew. My Mom sets a lot of rules. I hate it. When you have your own place, you can do as you please." She thought An apartment sounds better than a noisy dorm.

"I dunno," Buddy replied. "I wish someone cared whether I showed up someplace."

"I'd miss you terribly if you weren't in school," Cheryl replied, very carefully. "I look for you every day. It means a lot to me that we can eat lunch together."

"Same here," Buddy grinned. "I knew this was the right place to ask you to the Prom."

They went to the Prom and talked a lot because Buddy didn't dance well. Cheryl didn't mind, proud to be there in a long strapless dark red formal. She had seen a similar gown on a pop singer in a star-studded magazine with lots of pictures and bold-type paragraphs. Buddy brought her a wrist corsage of white roses. Everything was perfect. As they slow-danced, Buddy's cheeks were hot and moist against her own fevered skin. It was exciting to be that close to him. She was happier than she had been during the whole year. She would write to Valerie about the Prom, and not mention the Grecian Gardens.

During the next weeks, Cheryl met Buddy after school. He hung around her house, or she picked him up after work. They sat near the Sugar Maple for long hours and talked about the future. Buddy said he might become a department manager after graduation. Maybe he'd go to college someday after he got an apartment and a car.

Buddy leaned over, "I'll sure miss you when you're away at school."

Cheryl said, "We won't see each other until I come back at Thanksgiving." It seemed a very long time.

Buddy put his arm around her like he'd seen on television. "You're my only friend."

"Oh, Buddy, you're my best friend, too." She lifted her face close to his. She wasn't lonely with him around, but at the university, there'd be all new people. More loneliness. An apartment with Buddy would be a quiet oasis away from her Mom and Dad and these snobbish high school girls.

"Cheryl, I really love you. I really do." He cautiously kissed her once, twice, then lots more times.

"I love you, too!" Cheryl declared without hesitation.

"You're my girl. I really care about you."

"I've never had a real boyfriend before," Cheryl admitted.

"Will you wear my class ring? Then we could be really close."

To belong to him would be a wonderful feeling, Cheryl thought. "Gee, Buddy, I don't know . . ."

"We'll be like we're engaged. Other kids do it."

"What if I got pregnant . . .or AIDS?" What was the phrase? Know AIDS—No AIDS.

"You're safe with me. You know that I've never even dated anyone else."

"There's other things . . ."

"Cheryl! I'm clean! I love you. I won't let anything happen. Don't you love me? I just want my own place and YOU . . .YOU and me together. I want to BELONG to YOU."

Cheryl heard the desperation in Buddy's voice. She wanted to help him—to belong to him, too. She was confused. At church there were discussions in the youth group about abstinence. Before marriage, going all-the-way was wrong. Her parents had always admonished her to be a good girl. How could loving someone be wrong? Did sex make her a bad girl? Was there anything really sacred about sex? All the TV sitcoms and moves made hooking-up a lot of fun and the most important thing in the world. Wasn't hooking-up with someone you knew who didn't have AIDS better than to wait until you were older and left out?

Buddy asked again, "Cheryl, do you love me?"

"Oh, Buddy, I do—I do."

When Cheryl got home that night, she was troubled. Hooking-up wasn't like she expected. She thought that being loved meant a beautiful wedding with a long white dress and afterwards a trip to an exotic resort on Maui or Tahiti—a king-size bed with lovely white sheets and a full moon outside. It wasn't that way at all.

Instead, she could only remember a lot of fumbling and groping and the whole thing wasn't much fun, although she didn't tell Buddy this. Not the next day or the next week or the next month.

Three months later—before Cheryl was to leave for the university—she told Buddy that she was pregnant. He went with her to tell her mother. Her father was angry and stomped out of the room. Her mother cried.

Cheryl and Buddy were married the following Saturday by a Justice of the Peace. Her parents gave them a week at Disney World for a honeymoon and a six-month lease on an apartment near the freeway and Buddy's job.

Buddy's mother and Floyd gave them a check for a used car and Stewie sent his last child-support check directly to Buddy. Neither of Buddy's parents attended the brief ceremony.

A GALLON OF MILK

When Irma stepped out that morning to pick up The Times, she felt the slap of cold wind. Yesterday, she and Henry had raked the lawn—piling dead leaves high against the curb. Now the wind was sending them back across the dry grass. Irma's arms and shoulders still ached from her earlier effort. The leaves must be raked again.

Dear God, not today. I'm getting old. No, I AM OLD. But I won't think about that now. Today is a Museum Day. I'll have a good time. Life is fine. Everything is just fine—it has to be. I really count my blessings. Thank you, God.

After breakfast, Irma planned to shower and put on her beige suit—a shade too light for fall, but it still blended with autumn hues. She would wear the skirt, even though younger women would be in smart pant-suits with suede and leather trim and fancy boots to match. Myra, a newer Garden Club member, would pick her up at ten.

Irma took The Times inside and started breakfast. Automatically, she set out the cereal boxes, dropped bread in the toaster and poured orange juice. She pushed an ON button for the coffee maker and poured the last milk from a plastic jug into a pitcher. Henry could go to the store while she was gone. She hesitated. Perhaps she should go with him. No, that was foolish. Henry could certainly buy a gallon of milk by himself.

Irma hummed as she worked, anticipating a really good Museum day. She would see a Georgia O'Keeffe exhibit with canvasses of oversized blooms. Irma loved flowers. In

September, she had planted five dozen daffodils and ached for three days afterward. That didn't matter now because she could stand before O'Keeffe's originals and marvel at the way the artist captured the overwhelming wonder of a single blossom.

Please, dear God, don't let Ginger call and ask us to pick up her kids from school. Please, make this breakfast pleasant and easy. Please, at least today. Thank you, God.

When Henry padded in—his plaid house-slippers flapping at his heels—he wore only his shorts and undershirt. That wasn't like Henry. He was always so proper. Years ago at the bus stop, she first noticed his neat appearance. When he finally asked her to a movie, he wore a dark suit, white shirt and a maroon bow tie. Friends found his ties funny. They always teased him, but Irma liked the way it set Henry apart as someone who cared about his appearance.

Young men don't dress up for dates anymore. They wear those faded jeans and sweat shirts. But then, girls don't dress up either. No wonder there's no romance left in the world, she mused.

Irma shook her head at Henry. "You're not dressed."

"You call. I come," Henry grunted. "You don't like to wait. You say *Come while it's hot.* So here I am."

"I didn't make oatmeal this morning."

"You should have told me. I like oatmeal."

Irma sighed, "No matter—let's just eat. This is the last of the milk."

"Why didn't you get some? We always need milk."

Irma heard the grumpiness in his voice. Their sparring happened more often now. Would such snappishness get worse? Some old couples drifted apart—slept apart—even openly fought. They made everyone miserable at family celebrations.

Please, dear God, let us love each other during these last years. We've been through so much together—at least, help us to be pleasant to each other. Thank you, God.

"I'm going to the Museum today," Irma reminded Henry.

He didn't answer. He finished his cereal and picked up the newspaper. Some milk had dribbled down his chin. Irma reached over and tapped it lightly.

Henry reared back, "What are you doing?"

"You're holding the paper. You spilled. I only meant to help."

"You think I can't take care of myself? I'm not helpless!"

"No. No, of course not." Irma began to load the dishwasher.

Dear God, I know he's scared since his spell at church a month ago. Please give me patience. Let him know that all will be well. Thank you, God.

"Do you remember that I'm going with the girls today?" She reminded him. "To the Museum—with the Garden Club."

"Girls?" Henry joked. "Most are past fifty and the rest are in menopause."

Irma stared at him. Henry was a very proper man. Never one for a lot of words. He had been an accountant until he retired. Fortunately, he left just before his firm was sold to a conglomerate. She had never heard him say *menopause* before.

Irma laughed, "That's a new word for you."

Henry didn't answer, but turned The Times pages over and over as if he were hunting a special story. She wanted to ask, but decided against it. Maybe he missed his daily oatmeal and dry cereal confused him. She would remember to make oatmeal tomorrow; then he would be fine. In their bedroom, she laid out Henry's clothes—dark pants and a navy flannel shirt. He liked the warmth of flannel against his thin arms. She laid a pair of navy socks on top. What would he do while she enjoyed the Museum? Probably read and doze in his lounge chair.

Dear God, don't let him go down to the basement and use the jigsaw. That thing had been a birthday present from Ginger who wanted Henry to make a set of rock star figures for Taylor's bedroom. Where did Ginger get her ideas?

For a moment, Irma considered canceling her ride with Myra. No. Henry could drive the short distance to the supermarket for a gallon of milk. It would occupy some time until she returned. On this cold day, he would need a heavy sweater, so she laid out a bulky maroon one beside his other clothes. Then she showered with her favorite lavender soap and dressed for her day at the Museum.

Henry was still at the kitchen table with The Times when she was ready.

"I thought you'd be dressed," she said, cautiously.

Henry held the Sports Section, "I'm not going anywhere."

"Certainly not that way!" Irma replied. "I laid out your clothes. You can go to the supermarket today." Henry didn't answer, so she spoke more loudly. "It's almost nine-thirty, so get dressed. Now! At least, I'll know you're ready for the day."

Henry still sat there with the morning paper.

"It's a cold day," she said. "We're out of milk. Go to the store and pick up a gallon. Get skim or one percent." Henry didn't answer, so she asked, "Do you hear me?"

"I can't help but hear you. You've told me twice."

Irma stifled any laughter. Maybe Henry had a slight problem, but wasn't she forgetful, too? What did the experts say—there was no problem as long as you could remember the President's name and count backwards by seven.

Dear God, at least keep one of us healthy. Edward is dead. Where do we turn, if we both become ill?

Irma saw Myra pull into the drive in her Lexus. It gave Irma a thrill to ride in such a sleek dark blue car. Henry never spent money on a fancy car because he remembered

Depression poverty. Irma looked at Henry, still in his underwear. Quickly, she kissed the top of his head.

"I'm leaving. Don't forget about the milk."

Henry didn't look up, but he replied, "Have a good time. Don't spend all my money."

Irma laughed. That began a standard goodbye between them. "I'll just spend my half," she joked, "The rest I'll . . . . " she started to say burn but changed to " . . . eat."

Dear God, why am I so careful? What am I afraid of? It's ridiculous to be so wary of simple words.

She grabbed her coat, uncertain if she should have insisted that Henry be dressed before she left. Well, it was too late now. She dashed to the Lexus and greeted Myra with a smile.

"Don't you look nice!" Myra said, making small talk.

Irma was glad for the ride. Myra seemed too young to have a daughter Cheryl with a baby girl, Jennifer. Did people look younger or did babies come faster these days? Irma didn't pursue the question. Myra's husband was a vice-president at some company, always flying off to Europe. Last spring Irma met Myra at church and invited her to the Garden Club. Myra seemed pleased and offered to drive her to meetings.

Myra said, "I'm so glad that you came today. I was afraid you couldn't get away. I didn't know if you could leave Henry."

"Oh, Henry's just fine now. There's nothing wrong with Henry," Irma repeated.

Dear God, are people whispering behind our backs, because Henry fainted at church a month ago? Lots of people faint. It's nothing to worry about.

By the time the paramedics had come, Henry's color returned and his garbled mumbling's stopped. Later that week Henry was given a check-up. The doctor scheduled tests, but Henry couldn't get in right away. Irma wondered why everything in medicine took such a long time when so many new clinics and hospitals were nearby.

Dear God, Henry might be dead by the time the tests are done. Don't let that happen. Please.

Irma grew tired on the O'Keeffe tour. The docent had a soft voice, so Irma had a hard time hearing everything. The few flower pictures were fine, but there weren't enough of them. The artist's early sketches were fascinating, but then Irma's feet began to hurt. The galleries became hot and stuffy as other tour groups filled them.

Irma finished her chicken salad which had a lot of grapes and less chicken, but that didn't matter. It was good to sit there. The coffee was lukewarm, but the rainbow parfait was refreshing, so she felt better again. Irma silently prayed, Dear God, I'm so fortunate to be here. *Thank you for the nice day. And thank you for keeping Henry well so I could come.*

When they climbed into the Lexus, Myra's cell phone rang. Irma knew from the conversation, it must be Cheryl.

"Do you mind if we go out to the mall?" Myra asked. "Cheryl wants me to pick up Jennifer's proofs. It's hard to believe the baby is six months old! Cheryl's so anxious to see her latest pictures."

Quickly, Irma replied, "Just let me out at the supermarket." She could see Myra was relieved. "I'll call Henry. We need a gallon of milk and something for dinner. If he hasn't bought milk, I'll get it."

Myra passed her cell phone over to Irma so she could call Henry.

"Did you get the milk today?" Irma asked.

Henry answered slowly, deliberately. "I read the paper. And I watered your flowers."

Irma frowned. *Dear God, what does he mean? The flowers have already suffered a first frost. I cleaned up the garden two weeks ago.*

She spoke carefully to make sure that Henry understood her. "Henry, dear, pick me up at the supermarket. I'll get the milk and some chops for dinner. I'll be at the north entrance."

Henry answered, "Okay. Wait there. Be sure to get skim milk."

Irma wanted to laugh. Now Henry gave her directions. She went through the supermarket quickly, selected the meat, frozen vegetables and an apricot torte for dessert, which was Henry's favorite. She waited by the north door, ready to dash through the cold afternoon to Henry's waiting car. He took a long time.

Dear God, has he forgotten me? Keep him safe when he drives.

Maybe it was a mistake to call him. She spent time reading ads on the bulletin board. Finally, she saw Henry pull into a Handicap space at the south entrance. He got out and started for the entrance. *Dear God, he can't park there. He doesn't have a medical card—yet.* She needed to be quick so *that Security couldn't order him away.*

Irma was stunned. Henry wore a thin yellow summer shirt and bright blue sweat pants—clothing from the garage Goodwill bag. He was still in his floppy house slippers, without any jacket. He must be freezing. She rushed down the long aisle toward Henry. He headed to the dairy case and pulled out a milk jug.

Dear God, thank you for this sign. He remembered after all. Things are all right with Henry. I am grateful. Thank you. Thank you.

Henry looked surprised when he saw Irma. She showed him the groceries and milk, and he put his gallon back on a shelf. Henry drove slowly as they headed home. He passed their street, but he corrected himself at the next block.

Dear God, help me keep silent. Maybe he couldn't turn quickly enough to make the corner. It doesn't matter. We're home. We're safe. Thank you. Thank you.

Irma didn't ask about Henry's outfit. Maybe he intended to wash the car and found the old clothing in the garage. The day was really too cold for that. Maybe he wore them to water the garden. No, she must not question him right now. The warmth of their house hit Irma as she entered. A feeling of peace came over her.

Dear God, it's enough to be home. We're both safe and together. I won't ask for more. Thank you. Thank you.

Irma opened the refrigerator to put the groceries away. She stared hard. Four gallons of milk were crowded on the top shelf. Had Henry made four trips to the store? Or had he made one trip and bought four gallons? Irma slumped down with her gallon of milk. She wanted to believe everything was fine, but it wasn't. Nor would it ever be again.

Irma sobbed, *Dear God, what can I do?*

A SMALL JADE HORSE

When Cheryl first saw the small jade horse in the jeweler's window, she stood transfixed, breathless—her troubled brown eyes riveted in deep concentration. The figurine was centered in a black velvet alcove with soft light that enhanced its luminous green color. It glowed with a radiance from deep within the stone. Proudly, the little steed held its head high—nostrils flaring, a mane tumbling over the regal neck. One leg lifted as if it were prancing down some grand parade route. Instead, it was imprisoned in a shopping mall window.

Cheryl bent slightly and pressed her face hard against the cold glass. Her right hand slowly rubbed the glossy surface as if she might find a magic opening to reach in and touch the little horse. For a moment ancient temples with curving roofs of red and gold flashed through her mind.

Then Jennifer cried. Cheryl bent over her daughter's stroller. The baby, red-faced and rubbing sleepy eyes, had lost her pacifier. Cheryl pushed the dun-colored nipple between Jennifer's wailing lips. The child quieted, making small sucking sounds—the same noises that Buddy, Jennifer's dad, made when he sat with a soda.

Like father—like daughter, Cheryl thought with some guilt, pushing down—deep down—hidden anger over such crudeness. She knew Jennifer was tired. They'd been at the mall all morning. Cheryl didn't want it to end, because it was the one day a week when she could look at brightly colored displays. Everything was fresh and new and it lifted her spirit just to get away from their small dull cramped apartment.

Other women passed them and walked into the smart shops that Cheryl was afraid to enter. Their sleek shoes matched leather purses. They walked with such carefree confidence as they came out with large boxes and headed to their shiny cars. Cheryl sighed, knowing that she couldn't afford anything in any shop. As she pushed Jennifer down the long concourse, Cheryl saw the slim mannequins. She turned away when she noticed her own heavy reflection. Buddy grinned and called her *Pudgy.* She, in turn, called him *Fatso.* It was supposed to be funny, but it really didn't seem so now.

She circled the mall and returned to stare hard at the jade horse. She studied the fine carving, the lift of the head. Even the tail curved in perfect symmetry. Her eyelids narrowed as if the figurine were too bright for her dark eyes. She saw another girl come out of the jewelry store wearing a new gold bracelet. Cheryl felt her own eyes turning green—jade green—with envy. If that girl walked into the store, so could she. It wouldn't cost anything to look at the jade horse more closely.

Without hesitation, Cheryl pushed Jennifer's stroller through the open doorway. Immediately, she felt a hushed silence. Her worn sneakers seemed weighted and heavy on the thick beige carpet. Two women were seated fingering a tray of sparkling rings. They spoke in such muted tones that Cheryl couldn't hear them. A tall blonde woman, dressed in a tailored gray suit, came forward.

"May I help you?" the clerk asked, raising her eyebrows skeptically. A muscle along her left jaw tightened with stern patience. She was a middle-aged woman with pale blush cheeks and a heavy jaw. Everything about her was controlled.

Cheryl noticed the woman's neat chignon. In comparison, her own long black curls seemed childish and untidy. Her palms grew moist and her cheeks were red with embarrassment. Cheryl knew her jeans stretched too tightly across her hips—heavy with weight that remained from her pregnancy. Everything changed with Jennifer's arrival, she thought grimly. She expected to be free from her parents' rules when she and Buddy got married. Somehow, she didn't feel free at all.

Cheryl kept her eyes downcast, looking at a display of bright gems. With nervous fingers, she pulled at her faded Bambi T-shirt. Buddy bought a Donald Duck shirt on their honeymoon, too. She wished she were dressed in a white blouse and dark denim skirt.

"What are you interested in?" the clerk inquired, slightly frowning at Cheryl's awkward silence.

"Can . . . may I see that jade horse in the window?" Cheryl stammered, looking away and not meeting the clerk's wary eyes. Even within the store, the small jade horse seemed remote, faraway.

The clerk hesitated. "It's a beautiful piece, but I'd have to get a key for the window display. Are you interested in jade?"

Cheryl didn't know anything about jade. She knew that the clerk knew it, too. "Yes. Yes, I guess I am," Cheryl gulped, nervously biting her lower lip.

"It's an expensive piece," the clerk said, her slate-blue eyes coolly sweeping over the dirty shoes, the tight jeans, the faded shirt. She reached into a nearby case and pulled out a tray of pins. "This jade pin is beautifully classic. You could wear it with a scarf."

The clerk's voice trailed away as her hand swept up toward her long elegant neck. She poised the pin carefully on her lapel. Her fingernails were a pearly pink, a shade that blended with her pale silk blouse.

Cheryl looked down, hunching her shoulders together. She half-whispered, "How much is the horse?"

With an audible sigh, the clerk replaced the tray and locked the display case. Cheryl wanted to shout "I'm not a thief." Instead, she twisted a curl, knowing that she couldn't afford even a jade pin. The clerk knew it, too.

"The horse is six-hundred dollars!" the clerk snapped through thin taut lips. She moved toward a well-dressed man with a quick smile.

Cheryl, ignored, stood there awkwardly. Jennifer began to wail so she hurried out to the small parking lot. For once she didn't notice their old car's dented left fender or the driver's window that was half-rolled down. Automatically, she strapped Jennifer into her car seat, and drove to the apartment. Though other cars passed her, she saw only a spirited jade horse that pranced across a terrain of black velvet—a scene as dazzling as the hot noonday sun.

At home, Cheryl put Jennifer in her crib. She dialed her mother. "I saw a horse, a statue, at the mall this morning. Mom, it's so beautiful. It's a small jade horse."

Her mother didn't hear her. Instead, she asked "How's Jennifer? Make it quick. I'm on my way to a bridge benefit."

"Since I have a birthday soon . . . "

"It's a couple of months away!" Her mother answered, hurried and impatient.

"If you gave me a check now, I could put the jade horse on layaway. I'd pay something each month." Cheryl knew her voice sounded childlike because she was begging.

"Now, Cheryl! Your car needs new tires. There's Jennifer's doctor bill. You've got to be practical. Talk to you later."

"If you saw it . . . "

Cheryl heard her mother's quick click and the empty dial tone. She picked up a paperback about a Boston heiress, but the words were meaningless. The jade horse loomed before her eyes. If she owned it, she'd keep it on top of the bookcase away from Jennifer's and Buddy's hands. The bookcase was pressed wood and not worthy of such fine jade. She would get a job. She would buy a special lighted case. The figurine would stand regally above everything—her worn paperbacks and Buddy's racing car magazines. She could forget everything in the apartment if the little jade horse stood there near her.

When Buddy arrived, Cheryl sat opposite him on a gold plush sofa—one they bought at a highway outlet along with a waterbed. Sometimes her parents loaned them money when the monthly payments came due.

Today I saw a jade horse," she said, trying to interest Buddy. "The carving is so fine, so detailed."

Buddy half-listened as he flipped through an old magazine with a red car zooming across the cover. Cheryl thought he must have it memorized from the well-thumbed pages. His watery eyes were as dull as their gray bathroom tile. Cheryl knew even when Buddy grew old, his eyes would be the same. Eyes like that never saw anything. Buddy didn't see the wilted Boston fern. Or its macramé hanger that sagged, although it was strong enough for a person—a desperate person—to hang from it. Cheryl knotted her hands together.

"The horse is only so high." She spread her thumb and forefinger to illustrate.

Buddy didn't look up. He tossed the magazine aside. "Get Jennifer," he ordered in a macho voice. "I want to play with her NOW."

Silently, Cheryl obeyed, seeing how alike the baby and Buddy were with their moon-faces and thick eyelids. She wanted to feel a surge of love for both of them, but it didn't come. Somehow, Buddy, Jennifer and the dull apartment stood between her and the jade horse. Quickly, she left to shower, her salt tears mingling with the flowing water until she could control herself.

On the week-end, they went to the mall. Buddy carried Jennifer on his shoulders. Cheryl pushed ahead with hurried steps, half-afraid that the jade horse would be gone. However, it stood in the velvet alcove—alone, aloof, a commanding beauty.

"See!" Cheryl exclaimed. "Isn't it just beautiful . . . just beautiful?" Somehow the word didn't adequately describe it.

Buddy transferred Jennifer to his right hip, half-glancing toward the display. "It's awful small."

He pushed his face close to Jennifer's and made a guttural sound. The baby gurgled happily. Buddy repeated the noise as a long dreadlock fell down over his left eye. Jennifer squealed again and grabbed his hair. He slapped her hand.

Cheryl tried to interrupt. "Look at the proud head . . . the nostrils . . . the eyes . . . "

Jennifer cried. Buddy made a silly face at her.

"Don't you think it's quite remarkable?" Cheryl said louder.

"I guess so, if you're into rocks." Buddy pushed Jennifer toward Cheryl and walked away.

"It's not a rock!" Cheryl called. Buddy should understand that the jade's special glow came from an ancient fire that still burned within it. Like a pilgrim at a shrine, she stood there until Buddy motioned to her. She took one long last look, firmly fixing the jade horse in her mind. The display would be changed by the time she returned. Reluctantly, she followed Buddy to the car.

Two weeks later, Cheryl spooned carrots into Jennifer's mouth. Buddy walked in and the baby spluttered with delight so that small orange dribbles slid down her chin onto her clean bib. Cheryl reached for a washcloth.

"Look, Pudgy," Buddy said. He happily pushed a plaster horse at Cheryl. It was large, crude and white with a garish red and gold saddle. "You wanted a horse. I got you one. Shaun found this at a garage sale on Saturday." He grinned proudly with a sappy smile. "It cost me five dollars!"

Cheryl couldn't touch the horrid thing. Instead, she kissed Buddy lightly on the cheek. He pushed the horse into her hands anyway. She held it at arm's length as if she admired the bulky form. Buddy, pleased, reached into the refrigerator for a soda. As the door swung back, it touched Cheryl's elbow. The ugly horse fell to the floor. A rear leg and the tail shattered. Jennifer, startled, began to scream.

Buddy knelt down, fitting tail pieces against the horse's broad rump. "I can glue them together. It will hardly show," he added—still grinning, still pleased.

"No! It can't be fixed!" Cheryl snatched the pieces from him. She rushed from the apartment, away from Buddy's puzzled look and Jennifer's tiresome tears. She threw the broken pieces into a huge smelly trash bin. The ears and nose flew off, but the eyes peered up at her—mocking, smug, amused. She dropped the lid. It fell with a tinny bang that echoed down the long dark alley. Somewhere, an ambulance wailed in the starless night.

Cheryl knew that Buddy would never see—or know—the difference between the small jade horse and that piece of cheap plaster. They were not the same. They would never be the same. She stood there, defeated, crying as hard as Jennifer, with an even more terrible hunger.

LOVE THY NEIGHBOR

Myra would always associate Gene's call from London with the arrival of their new neighbor.

"I'll take the midnight flight and be home tomorrow," he said. "Don't plan anything. Negotiations have been hard. I want a quiet week-end." He paused, "Have you heard from Cheryl?"

Their daughter Cheryl and Buddy were expecting a second baby any time. Buddy was an army Corporal, stationed at Ft. Lewis, Washington. Myra had her bag packed, ready to leave when the baby was born.

"No." Myra saw their new neighbor walk toward their entrance. "We have another family next door," she said a little loudly, as if to bridge the Atlantic more easily. "I saw two boys and a dog."

Gene groaned. "We don't need kids and a dog tearing up the lawn. They'll want to borrow the mower and the snow-blower . . . whatever." Gene was relieved when the previous family with teen-age twin girls moved away.

"Oh, don't be an old grumpy Grandpa!" Myra laughed, quickly wishing she'd said something else. "It'll be fun to pass out Halloween treats. Maybe they're Cub Scouts and will sell us Christmas wreaths."

"You're always the good neighbor. Let's keep our distance."

Myra hung up as the doorbell rang. Her new neighbor stood there, carrying a little girl on her hip. The child buried her head in her mother's shoulder when she saw Myra.

"Hi!" said the young woman. "I'm Stephanie. This is Madison . . . Maddie, for short. May I borrow some glass cleaner? I forgot to get a bottle at the supermarket."

Myra led them into the kitchen and handed a half-full bottle to Stephanie. "Keep it," she said. She wondered if the cleaner wasn't an excuse to get acquainted. She handed a cookie to Maddie, who wore a yellow sunsuit with an appliquéd blue bunny.

"Say *Thank you* to . . . ?"

"Myra." She noticed Stephanie's slim long legs, her brief denim shorts and a *Save the Earth* shirt that clung to her model-thin body.

"What a beautiful old-fashioned name," Stephanie smiled. "You're an awfully good neighbor to help me out."

"I try to be." Myra changed the subject. "Our daughter is having a second baby soon. If she has another girl, I'll hunt for a sunsuit like Maddie's."

"Oh, little Maddie has lots of sunsuits! We came from Santa Barbara," Stephanie offered. "I have two boys. Brett is nine and Travis is six. Maddie is almost three. And we have a terrier MacIver . . . Mac for short." She gave a brief laugh. "That's the little family next door to you. We've leased for a year."

"Was your husband transferred here?"

"No. I'm divorced. I came back to hometown roots. Divorce does that." Stephanie shifted edgily, her lips in a thin taut line. "I left my ex in Santa Monica. On the beach with his surfboard. He liked to spend my inheritance! Next time, I'll find a solid citizen with MONEY." She added with a hollow laugh. "I need help with my three kids."

"There aren't any eligible men in this neighborhood," Myra replied.

"I'll meet someone. I'm ready to marry again." Stephanie tossed her dark pony tail with confidence.

Myra touched her own hair which was short and gray.

However, even with a silver rinse, it seemed drab compared to Stephanie's long shining hair. Myra decided that next time she'd try a new cut.

In the hallway, Stephanie picked up a picture of Cheryl and Gene taken before Cheryl moved to the Pacific coast. "Your kids?"

Myra hesitated. Surely, Stephanie realized that it was a father-daughter photo. Quickly, she said, "No, that's Cheryl and her Dad. My husband does look young. He tries to keep fit."

Gene complained about graying sideburns. He exercised on a basement treadmill as well as at the athletic club. He wanted two-year-old Jennifer to call him *Poppy* instead of *Grandpa*. Gene was definitely afraid of growing old.

Myra didn't reveal any of this to Stephanie. Instead, she said, "He plays golf to stay in shape."

Stephanie's eyes widened. "Really? I love golf. I brought my clubs with me. We'll have to play together sometime."

"He's very busy," Myra murmured as Stephanie and Maddie exited the front door. Why did she feel unsettled by Stephanie? Whenever Myra wanted to ease tension, she weeded her perennial bed. She spent almost an hour among the Shasta daisies and delphiniums.

Two nights later as Myra and Gene finished dinner, the door bell rang. Brett, white-faced and teary-eyed, stood there.

"Have you seen Mac? I'm to watch him, but he got away. I can't find him anywhere." Brett's voice trembled.

Myra thought the kid looked cute in his concern. "I'll help you. We'll drive around. Wait here while I get my keys."

Gene came up behind her. "I tell you . . . don't get involved!"

"He's so young. He needs help."

She and Brett drove several blocks when they spied Mac

barking at a cat up a tree. When Brett called, the dog ran and jumped into his arms. Brett nuzzled his pet while Myra drove home. She had a warm feeling about her effort. She was surprised to see Gene and Stephanie together on the driveway.

"Gene is telling me about London," Stephanie smiled. "To think that he finally saw *The Mousetrap*."

Myra looked at him. Nothing had been said about a theater night. Gene implied that only business occupied his time. That's why he came home so tired. Oh well, he deserved to relax once in awhile. Gene reddened. "It was a late-night performance."

Stephanie continued, "I spent a junior semester at Kingston College. I love London. So wonderful! I got into Christie and all that. Even a class in Shakespearean sonnets."

"London has a lot of glass and steel now," Gene said smoothly.

"You must tell me more about it." Stephanie put her hand lightly on Gene's arm. "I'd love to go back . . . even for a long week-end. Next time, just tuck me in your bag. I won't cause trouble."

Gene moved slightly away and Stephanie dropped her hand. "No more overseas trips for awhile. I'm staying home."

"That's great!" Stephanie smiled. "I always feel safer with a good man around." She gave a little wave and led Brett and Mac toward their house.

Gene called after her, "Let me know if you need anything."

Inside, Myra half-teased, "Now, aren't you the one getting involved with our new neighbor?"

"Involved? I said, if she needed some little thing . . . "

". . . Which she'll find." Stephanie's kind always managed to find an excuse.

"You're the one who always wants to help other people. You took the kid to hunt for the dog!"

"He needed help! You said you were tired and wanted to go to bed. Jet-lag."

Myra knew that somehow they were quarreling. She was surprised how quickly it erupted. She was glad when the phone rang.

"You have a new grandson named Jeremy," Buddy exclaimed. "Cheryl and the baby are fine. How soon can you come?"

"My bag is packed." Myra said gaily. "See you tomorrow!"

Before they went to bed that night, Gene ran his hand through his hair and asked, "Do you think I'm getting bald?"

"No way," Myra reassured him. She did not call him *Grandpa*.

On the way to the airport, Myra's taxi passed the Sugar Maple. She glanced at the green leaves, now brushed with gold and scarlet—an early hint of fall. She didn't intend to be away for more than two weeks, but one never knew with babies. If Cheryl needed her, she would stay longer. By the time she returned, the Maple would be even more brilliant. Or late summer heat might deaden the leaves and turn them brown to be easily crunched underfoot. Nature was never static. This bothered Myra—a premonition of some unforeseen trouble ahead. Things never stayed the same. She thought the secret of life was to embrace each season and enjoy it. Now she wasn't sure. Was she too adaptable? Did she accept change too easily?

Myra was gone for three weeks. She called Gene nightly. Sometimes she didn't reach him. One night he mentioned that he had been at Stephanie's for dinner.

"We talked a long time about golf. She attended the last PGA tournament. Her kids are really cute and well-behaved." He sounded pleased. "Stay as long as you're needed. I'm getting along fine."

Myra didn't want to hear that. As she rocked Jeremy, she thought about the conversation. It was time to go home.

At the airport, Myra arrived on an earlier flight. She planned to surprise Gene and have a light supper ready when he arrived home. As she passed the Sugar Maple, she gasped. While she was gone, it had changed to autumn colors. It glowed in the late summer sun, a fiery scarlet with glints of orange and gold. It was like a seductive dancer, demanding attention even as cars sped by.

As the taxi pulled up, Myra noticed their garage door was open. Gene's green convertible was parked inside. For a moment, she felt a slight panic. Perhaps he was ill and had come home early. In the hallway, she called "Gene", but there was no answer. She only heard the grandfather clock ticking and the echo of her own voice as she ran upstairs. Maybe Gene had fallen asleep. No, the bed was empty and unmade. A blanket was thrown across a chair. She folded it up. The room was dark, so she pulled aside the drapes.

She looked down into Stephanie's backyard. There was Gene, standing at the grill with a striped chef's apron. Where did he get that? From Stephanie? He wore navy blue shorts that Cheryl had given him for his birthday two years before. They were left in a bottom drawer because he didn't like the shade.

Stephanie stood beside Gene—her long legs emphasized again in brief pink shorts. A matching tank top clung to her firm breasts. She opened a can of beer for Gene and one for herself. They tapped their cans together in a mock salute. Maddie pulled at Gene's leg. He reached down and tossed her up in the air. The child clapped her hands for a repeat performance. Gene lifted her high several times while Maddie giggled. Myra thought, *If he complains about his back tomorrow, it will be hard to keep silent.*

Myra realized that their mower stood near Stephanie's

back door. Her neighbor's grass was freshly cut. When Gene complained about their own grass, Myra hired a lawn company. Evidently, Gene had changed his mind about yard work—or Stephanie had changed it for him.

Myra went outside and crossed to the fence that separated the two yards. "I'm back!" she gaily called, her voice a bit too high-pitched.

Both Stephanie and Gene looked surprised. Brett and Travis quit tossing a stick to Mac. The dog followed them to stand at the fence with Stephanie and Gene who still had Maddie in his arms.

"I caught an earlier flight," Myra continued.

Gene stammered, "Stephanie invited me, so I came home early." He pointed to the grill. "She needed help with the barbeque."

"Gene's such a good neighbor," Stephanie said smoothly. "He offered to cut the grass. He wouldn't let me pay him, so I insisted that he eat with us. At least that!"

Gene turned to Stephanie, "Mowing the lawn is the LEAST I could do when the boys watered Myra's garden while she was gone."

"You're such a good neighbor," Stephanie patted him on the shoulder and let her hand gently glide down his back.

Myra looked at the five of them—six, with Mac—across the fence. They made a family picture that could be put on a Christmas card. Then she noticed that Gene's hair had turned a lighter brown. His graying temples were gone, too. Was a new hair color his idea or Stephanie's? Had other things changed in her absence?

"There's plenty of food if you care to join us," Stephanie continued.

"Another time." Myra turned away without looking back.

She went upstairs and sat motionless, thinking about Stephanie and Gene. She didn't open her suitcase. She heard the grandfather clock chime the evening hour. The clock was always there to mark passing time, she thought ruefully. Perhaps her time had ended. Things were not right if Gene lied to his office staff and spent an afternoon with Stephanie.

Myra waited for Gene to return. When she heard his footsteps, she quickly slipped into the bathroom and closed the door. Instead of a shower, she turned on the tub spigots full force and poured in some gardenia scented gel—the kind her mother once used. She watched the foam bubble higher and higher.

She looked in the wide mirror and studied her own reflection, noting the deepened crow's feet around her puzzled eyes. Slowly, she undressed and slipped into the silky warm water. She sponged her upper arms and realized they were really quite flabby. She moved the washcloth over her legs. First, she lifted her right leg, then the left. Up and down. Up and down. She knew—even if she scrubbed harder and stretched them even farther—her aging legs would never be long and sleek.

NINE-ELEVEN

Before Gene left for New York City on Monday morning, he stepped into the back yard to take one last glance at Myra's garden. Myra spent long hours on her flowers. They looked so lovely. Bumblebees covered the rose and lavender fall asters. The golden Rudbeckia stood like small sunflowers centered with chocolate buttons. Even the late daylilies seemed especially large with green ribs on creamy petals. The summer months had gone so quickly. Gene pushed away guilty thoughts that he didn't take time to fly west to see his daughter Cheryl and the new baby. Her hasty marriage two years ago and Jennifer's quick birth still irritated him. He didn't like to think about Buddy, her husband.

Where had the summer gone?   Gene wondered. As he turned toward the garage for his car, Stephanie came across the grass. He didn't expect to see his neighbor because she had Brett and Travis to send off to school. Stephanie wore a T-shirt with an Art Museum logo and brief beige shorts. She looked good. Her legs looked very good. They always did. She was one of the few women who looked good in tight jeans, too.

"I had to see you before you left," Stephanie said with an inviting smile. "Brett says there's a spaghetti dinner next Friday to raise money for a Scout week-end. The Dads will help. He wants you to go with him."

Gene hesitated. He'd been with Stephanie and the kids a lot while Myra was gone. It was routine to treat her kids to ice cream at night. They'd pile in his convertible and he'd drive through darkened streets to a teen-age ice-cream hangout. Somehow the neon lights and cars with their radios booming made him feel light-hearted, younger. Stephanie sat by him with her bright red lips and long hair flowing to her shoulders. It reminded him of a time—too long ago—when he and Myra treated Cheryl's friends to ice cream on summer nights. Why didn't their years with Cheryl last longer?

"I'm not sure," Gene said evasively, "I may be back in London." It wasn't true, but it postponed a decision. How could he explain to Myra that he wanted to help at a Scout spaghetti dinner when he wouldn't attend a church chili supper with her?

Stephanie gave a quick pout. "If you're gone, he'll understand." Then she winked and smiled warmly. "I know you won't let him down." She took a deep breath. "He'll miss you. I'll miss you. It'll be too long until you get back."

Gene heard her intimate tone. "I'll be back Wednesday night. I'll let Brett know then."

"If this fence weren't here, I'd give you a hug for good luck. I hope things go well in New York. Please call me tonight . . . just to let us know you're okay. Even if it's late. Promise?" She blew him a kiss and dashed back across her lawn.

Gene looked toward the kitchen window to see if Myra had watched Stephanie's quick gesture. During the summer, Myra had grown distant toward Stephanie's family while he'd become more involved. He enjoyed Brett's pitching at Little League games.

A strange thing happened at the championship game a week ago when Brett pitched a no-hitter. During the seventh inning stretch. Maddie, who was seated between Stephanie and him, wanted popcorn.

"Here's a dollar." Gene gave Maddie a bill. "Don't eat it all before you get back. Your Mom and I want some," he teased.

Maddie giggled and ran off waving her bill.

Stephanie called, "Tell Daddy-Gene *Thank-you*." She moved closer to Gene and her face brushed his shoulders. "So much for teaching manners. I try!"

"You're doing fine," he smiled.

"It's not easy to be alone." She put her hand lightly on his arm. "I depend on you—maybe too much. Your strength gives me strength."

At that moment, the opposing pitcher's mother came toward them.

"We meet again," she said to Stephanie. "You must be proud of Brett. He's pitching a really good game." She nodded to Gene. "I'm Gayle. You must be Brett's Dad."

Gene's face reddened. "No . . . just a neighbor."

Gayle, embarrassed, murmured, "My mistake." She hurriedly left.

"That's a compliment!" Stephanie gaily replied. "You look young enough to be even Maddie's Dad!"

Gene looked away. It was nice to be considered young, when he was the grandfather of two. Little stabs of guilt crowded his thoughts. He didn't think as much about Cheryl and her kids as he should. He didn't want to think about Buddy, his son-in-law. Maybe the army would send Buddy overseas, and he wouldn't see him for a long time. Buddy had made a mess of Cheryl's life.

Gene was surprised when a stranger extended his hand. "I'm Tony Carlson. Aren't you Gene, Myra's husband? I sing with Myra in the Civic chorus. What brings you here?"

"My neighbor's kid is pitching. This is his mother, Stephanie."

Tony nodded and asked, "Myra's not here?"

"She's not interested in Little League games."

"Tell Myra *Hi* from me. I'm a tenor in the back row. Nice to meet you." He gave Gene and Stephanie a quizzical look before he turned away.

Gene felt uncomfortable, but Stephanie laughed, "There'll be whispers! You're out with a divorcee and her kids."

"He was surprised to see me among this young crowd."

Stephanie tossed her head. "You fit in beautifully. You can't deny that you do look young." Her hand slid down into his palm and lingered there. It was warm and light—an intimate touch as if they were ready to shake hands on some unforeseen agreement.

Gene was silent. *I want to believe you.* He pushed away thoughts about his hair coloring and that his teeth were professionally whitened. Stephanie had never seen him in his old slippers and faded blue jogging suit which were so comfortable padding around the house on a cold winter night.

Gene dropped her hand and turned toward the game, aware that others watched them, too. How had he slipped into this relationship with Stephanie? It was easy for him to confide in her—things like rumors of a company shake-up. He didn't want to worry Myra with office problems, but he wanted to talk to someone away from the office. Stephanie was available. Her confidence in him was appealing.

She would murmur sympathetically, "You're too important to be cut! I wish my ex had been concerned about his job. He thought he could run a scuba shop. Ha! He knew nothing about business. You do!"

He stayed late after the ball game. He explained to Myra, "The kids wanted one game of Hearts, too. I'm a father-figure. Isn't that what experts say that kids need? If their own Dad isn't around, then others must step in. You said yourself, they're cute kids."

Myra countered, "Their uncle lives across town. Stephanie should ask her brother to help her."

"Stephanie wants my guidance."

Myra snapped, "She wants more than that!" She hurried upstairs to take a bath.

Gene wondered *What is ahead? Myra's upset because I*

spend time with Stephanie. Why is it wrong when Stephanie makes me feel so alive? I can't—I won't give her up.

That Monday morning Gene was relieved to fly off to New York City, away from the tension between Myra and him. In comparison, Stephanie was always so vibrant, so grateful while Myra grew more wary. It was his wife's fault if she didn't trust him. Yes, it was Myra's fault if she were jealous.

Gene enjoyed his escape. In the cool crisp fall air, the big metropolis excited him with the honking taxis and smartly dressed people. Gene's afternoon business meeting was intense. The company's latest promotional videos were missing—sent to Atlanta instead of New York — so Gene's meeting was rescheduled for Tuesday afternoon. In his hotel room, he found scarlet lilies with a card that read *Just for You.* It was a Stephanie gesture—overdone, but one to make sure that he thought of her. He started to call her, but hung up. No reason to give her that attention without calling Myra, too. It was hard to talk to Myra now.

Instead he called Bruce, his old college roommate. Could they meet somewhere? Bruce invited Gene to his office in the North Tower the next morning—ninety-fourth floor, turn left, third office. Gene agreed. When he fell asleep, his last thoughts were of Myra's garden earlier that morning and Stephanie's blown kiss.

On Tuesday morning—September, the eleventh—Gene never felt more confident. His shower zinged every pore on his fit body, and he knew he was alive for a great day. It would be successful if the CEO approved the advertising campaign for next spring. To be tapped for a promotion, one always stayed ahead of the game. His attaché case was filled with pages of his carefully prepared report. He patted it for good luck. It promised to be a very good day.

He dressed carefully. His fall suit blended with his hair

coloring. He wore the muted rust tie that Stephanie gave him as a *thank-you* for hanging a picture in Maddie's room. He slipped his wallet, filled with his gold and platinum credit cards into his breast pocket. No pickpocket could get at them. He had everything he needed. He felt successful. He was a success. Gene skipped breakfast, knowing that Bruce would have coffee and rolls for him. He nodded to the hotel maid and smiled at the doorman as he left. He tipped the taxi driver an extra bill when they arrived at the Twin Towers. Life was very good.

Gene stared up at the vertical giant. Magnificent. Someday, he might work in the Twin Towers, too, if he made it to the top—not if but how soon? No more crabgrass and Whittimore. He pushed through the heavy glass doors and took an elevator to the forty-ninth floor. He turned left and realized at the third office that he was in the wrong place. Did Bruce say forty-ninth or ninety-fourth? He turned back to the elevator.

At that moment, Gene heard a terrible grinding thunder. The Tower shook. An earthquake? A young man dashed into the hall. "Don't worry, the building's safe!" He ran on calling out "Stay inside". Others poured out of their offices. With puzzled faces they asked, "What's happening? Do you know anything? I won't stay here! Not me!"

They rushed toward the stairs.

Gene was confused. The elevator didn't stop. A middle-aged woman in a black suit and stiletto heels kicked off her shoes as she ran toward the red EXIT sign. "Get out!" she screamed. People pushed Gene along. He tried to turn around. Someone fell against him and knocked his attaché case to the floor. He reached down to retrieve it, but more people spun him around and propelled him ahead.

"My papers! My report!" Gene yelled, buffeted by the throng, now at the stairwell.

Some guy behind him yelled out, "Your life! Get out!

Save your life!"

Others pushed him forward. "Down the stairs, man! Down!"

The noise and confusion grew larger. Bells rang. People screamed. At that moment the North Tower shook, tilted, swayed. Forty-first floor. He stumbled. Someone stepped on his foot. Gene knew he was doomed . . . a mere speck in a growing mass of people tumbling down the stairwell. He smelled smoke. He threw away his tie, so he could breathe. Thirty-eighth floor. He would be crushed when the building fell, dead in a steel and concrete tomb. Twenty-second floor. Firemen rushed up the stairwells against the crowd. Were they mad? Go faster, faster. Eleventh floor. Down. Down. Don't stop.

A girl falls. People step on her. No one stops. Keep counting. More grinding crashing noise. Somehow, he reached the ground floor, the mob thrusting him forward.

A concrete boulder smashed a wall. Gene saw an opening through the shattered glass. He plunged through—others behind, around and ahead of him. Run. Run harder. He threw off his jacket. Wailing sirens and fire trucks came at him. Run faster. More crashing glass. People falling from the sky. Run faster. Faster like others beside him. Faster. Faster. A blast of intense heat hits him. Paper and grit cling to him. White ash could bury everyone. Suddenly Gene stopped. He couldn't run farther, so he trudged along with the growing throng, covered now with falling white paper—floating bits turned into office confetti. The somber crowd moved like shrouded ghosts in some old black and white movie.

Gene didn't know how far he'd walked. He didn't look back. This was the end of everything. He heard the noise of doom—blaring horns, shrill whistles, wailing sirens, clanging alarms, bonging bells, great crashing booms, and a massive gray-white mushroom cloud expanding in the clear blue sky. The whole city was being destroyed. Sodom and Gomorrah.

He could not look back.

When he came to Union Square, Gene threw himself down on the grass and wept, exhausted—an ashen heap amid confusion. He realized he had nothing. His attaché case was gone. He had no wallet, no money, no credit cards, no airplane ticket. Nothing. Nothing. He had escaped death. He was alive—for what?

Myra! I must get home to Myra , he thought. *Myra will know what to do*. She always had a kind word, a soothing hand. Maybe it had something to do with going to church and saying prayers. If he had died, Myra would weep. Cheryl, too, would cry for him. He must do something for Cheryl and her children—even Buddy. But Myra—it was Myra. He really needed Myra.

It was the end of his world. Gene wept.

Five days later, Gene sat in Myra's garden, to recuperate in the peace and quiet. His hands trembled as he tried to recover from Nine-Eleven. Sometimes, he heard a deep grinding noise and crashing glass in his fretful sleep. Maybe he would hear it forever. The aroma of Queen Elizabeth roses as yet couldn't overcome the smell of acrid air that stayed with him. He studied Myra's flowers which seemed even more brilliant than before he left. Their beauty quieted him.

Stephanie came across the grass and stood beside him. She wore another Stephanie outfit—denim shorts and a bright red top with a white belt—red, white and blue in a burst of patriotism. Somehow, she looked childish—like a too-old pop-star, blind to her age.

She reached down to hug him. "O-o-oh," she crooned, "the kids were all so worried about you. Maddie cried over Daddy-Gene in the Twin Towers. And I . . . I can't imagine life without you."

Gene shook off her hug. "The world will never be the

same," he said quietly. "My friend Bruce died." He studied Myra's red geraniums intently, and repeated, "Bruce died."

"Tell me what happened."

"You've seen television. I have nothing to add." He turned away. He wanted to be free of Stephanie. She should hit on someone her own age. She'd find someone else.

Gene knew he looked different. He showered twice a day, trying to wash away the disaster's smoky grit which he felt still clung to him. With his tint gone, his hair was more gray and thin on top. He didn't care if he appeared old, slumped there in his worn slippers and old jogging suit. His world had changed forever. Bruce and thousands—how many?—were dead. Why did they die? Why did he live?

Myra came from the house with a glass of ice tea for Gene. "Oh, Stephanie, I didn't realize that you were here."

Gene reached for Myra's hand. "Get a lawn chair from the garage. Sit with me."

Stephanie followed Myra. "Gene won't talk to me," she said.

"His nerves are shattered. Bruce, his college roommate, was killed. The doctor says that Gene needs rest and quiet. It's something like battle-fatigue." Myra paused. "Your concern is sweet, but it will be better if we're alone for awhile. Gene's sister Cam is coming from Akron. Cheryl and the children will arrive later."

Stephanie hesitated "If there's anything I can do . . ."

"Nothing." Myra felt confident—in charge of everything. Stephanie's life had been changed by Nine-Eleven, too. Myra knew she and Gene were free of their neighbor.

Myra sat beside Gene. They held hands in silence. A Monarch butterfly lingered on a golden Rudbekia. Somewhere a hummingbird circled a rose coneflower..

"Beautiful," Gene murmured. "Your garden is so beautiful. It's good to be here with you."

He lifted Myra's left hand to his lips and gently kissed her wedding ring.

GINGER GETS RELIGION

It wasn't only Nine-Eleven that put me on the Right Path. On that awful morning my horoscope read *It is time to feed your soul. You need spiritual nourishment. Seek a spiritual advisor*. There it was in black and white. With the world falling down around me, Stewie went off on another sales trip. (Was it necessary or one for his convenience? I didn't ask.) I just knew that my horoscope was a warning that I might not have much time left. I had to *Get Right with God*.

I was glad Stewie was gone for the whole week because I didn't have to explain my sudden interest in church. I called Irma who never quit going—even with Eddie's death and Henry in a nursing home. How could she be thankful? She just said softly, *I know the Lord watches over us*. He sure didn't watch over New York City or do much for her, but I was real polite and didn't point that out.

Anyway, I thought I ought to be dressed in black, so I bought a new printed blouse with butterfly sleeves and a black straw hat. I looked real presentable. I could have left the hat at home, because I was the only one there except a retired preacher's wife who wore a black cloche that didn't even have a flower.

Irma chose the nine a.m. service because it had a Praise Band. That meant two guitars, a sax, a drum and a keyboard. The songs were up on a big screen, and I really got into the beat, clapping my hands and swaying like I'd been there every Sunday. It seemed like it would be real easy to be spiritual. I felt good.

We sat in the back, because I said I might have to go to the Ladies. Then a lady stood up to read from the Bible. She said, "Today, we focus on the E-Pistol to the Romans." I waited, because she didn't read about any gun. I didn't know the Romans carried them anyway. It didn't make sense so I went to the Ladies and filed my nails.

Irma sat real still to listen to the sermon. The preacher had a nice voice and spoke right up about *Grace* and *Saint Teefee Cajun*. I expected a real good story about how they found God having a good time. Instead, he read a Jesus story from the Bible and that confused me more. I knew right then that church wasn't for me. I went to the Ladies again and fixed my mascara. I never did find out about Grace and Saint Teefee, but they sang a song about amazing Grace. What was she into that was so amazing? Besides I never was blind. I can see perfectly well. When the offering time came, Irma put in a bill for me and I will say my ex mother-in-law acts like a good Christian.

When church was over, I told Irma that I would have to find my own spiritual nourishment. "I didn't understand what was going on or what the preacher said."

Irma answered, "If you come often enough, you'll find out. The church has a language of its own just like musicians or scientists. Words like Grace and Sanc-ti-fi-cation mean a lot to believers. If you're a child of God and belong to him, worship helps you to keep on living—no matter what happens."

I thanked her kindly. I told her that Lance liked Sunday School so she could pick him up. Besides, it always gives me a little peace and quiet, since he and Tyler fight over Sunday morning cartoons. I told Stewie to get everyone a TV. Then Stewie can watch his games, I'll see movies, and each kid chooses whatever.

I knew I had to find a spiritual advisor, so I looked in the yellow pages. Because of Nine-Eleven, I wanted someone who was a true-blue American. Let me tell you there were pages of churches of every kind—some with big bold letters, pictures of preachers and their wives, crosses, crowns, maps with dots. It was as confusing as the names—New Creation, Crossways, Saint's Rest, True Love (I almost went there), Angels or Apostles (what's the difference?). Even one called Up Yonder. I expected Wild Blue Yonder, too, but perhaps that's too patriotic to be spiritual. All I wanted was to talk to someone.

It was Divine Intervention (as Shepherdess Moriah later said) when I read the advertisements posted on the supermarket bulletin board. There was an invitation—WELCOME to the FELLOWSHIP of the DIVINE FLOCK—Meets Thursday nights at the Westside Mall Community Room. Refreshments at 6:30 p.m. Response at 7 p.m.

I didn't know what that Response business meant—if we were to tell them how we liked the refreshments, but I thought I'd give it a try. Right away, I knew that this was the place I belonged. When I walked in, a few people stood around, but two black women smiled at me, just as if I were expected. My voice got all fluttery, and I asked if I was in the right place. Shepherdess Moriah came and put her arm around me. She said, "Yes, and you will be our latest lamb. Come into our fold. We've been waiting for you."

"Really? I want to visit tonight," I replied.

"Of course! Help yourself to cheese and crackers. There's cider, orange juice or cocoa." She paused, "We never serve liquor because we're not allowed to do that here. Clean living is one of our beliefs." I didn't know exactly what that meant. Could I have a margarita on Mexican night at The Toledo restaurant? However, Stewie and I seldom go there anymore, so that business about Clean Living was okay by me.

Finally, we sat down in a big circle and closed our eyes for Meditation. Shepherdess Moriah turned on a boom box with Indian flute music which calmed us to be open to the Divine Aura that would soon surround us. She turned down the lights and lit seven cinnamon candles which filled the room with a spicy scent. Believe it or not, I relaxed and felt more peaceful than I had for many weeks. I didn't even think of Stewie or the kids once.

In a musical voice, Shepherdess Moriah read to us about a lovely light by some Edna Saint Millie, and a guy named Robert Floss who drove his horses through the woods when he was sleepy. Sounded dangerous to me. She said during the fall season we would listen to American writers, since Nine-Eleven alerted us to get back to our roots.

I wanted Shepherdess Moriah to know that I knew something about saints, so I asked if she had any readings by Saint Teefee Cajun. She shook her head and gave me a strange look, so I said I thought he was a Native American and probably wrote in sign language. She smiled and asked how I liked the readings. I said that guy named Floss should have listened to his wife, because she would have told him to take the main road when it snowed.

Then came a period of silence when we were to think of one good thing that happened that day. I tried hard. I remembered that Lance didn't spill his milk at breakfast. I was glad for that. Without warning, a young Asian with a crew cut and a university sweater stood up. "I need to make a confession."

That really scared me. I couldn't tell about drinking alone when Stewie didn't come home until after midnight. What was something that I'd done that wasn't real bad? I remembered my new sandals! I bought them after Stewie and I quarreled. He said I must quit buying things on impulse. The sandals were gold-colored—perfect with my black velvet pants. I paid cash and hid them in the basement closet behind the kids' winter boots, so he wouldn't find them. I looked around. I was sure the Divine Flock would understand.

Confession time turned out differently from anything I expected. We pushed our chairs into smaller circles called Sheepfolds. We introduced ourselves by first names. Then we took turns. Sandy, a teen-ager, said she cheated on a test. This meant Going down the Wrong Path. Across the circle, middle-aged Leland told about his good deed. He paid for a street-person's lunch. This meant Going on the Right Path. They exchanged places, so Sandy could absorb positive feelings from Right Path's chair. Leland, in turn, sat in her chair to overcome the negative vibrations left there. What was a Right Path testimony for me? Finally, I remembered that I car-pooled Taylor's friends to their dance class, and it wasn't even my day. So I told that after my gold-shoe confession.

By the time we finished, there were lots of exchanged chairs and laughter. The room was filled with positive hugs because everyone was on the Right Path. Then they put two bills apiece in the Feed My Sheep bowls—one for other Lost Sheep and one to help those in the Fold. I didn't have money with me, but Shepherdess Moriah said I could bring my money next time. I felt so good when I left, because Shepherdess Moriah understood me. The other Lambs also listened which was more than Stewie ever did. I went home that night and I slept better than any time since Nine-Eleven.

The next week I became a Lamb and joined the Fellowship of the Divine Flock. When Shepherdess Moriah dipped her finger in a silver bowl and made a circle on my forehead, I knew I was a Lamb forever, and safe in the Sheepfold. Everyone hugged me and Sandy and I both cried for joy. No one bothered me with committee work or singing strange hymns or listening to sermons. Everyone was friendly, like we were a real family.

I told Stewie, "I need a Sheepfold in our backyard so I can meditate with other Lambs and stay on the Right Path."

He snapped back, "I don't want your smelly sheep in my

backyard!"

Stewie doesn't understand our Divine Flock because he will never be a Lamb. He is one stubborn RAM!

BETWEEN FLIGHTS

Stewie didn't feel good. He slept in the den because his restlessness disturbed Ginger. The sales division was being reorganized. Older reps—like himself—had been reassigned to smaller territories. The oldest salesmen were given early retirement. He couldn't afford that—not with three kids to send to college. Thank goodness, his oldest son Buddy had a career in the army. Already he was a Staff-Sergeant in an armored division.

It wasn't only his job that worried Stewie, but Ginger's latest demand. Now that she was a Lamb, she wanted a Sheepfold—really a meditation room copied from some fancy Arizona spa. Cedar with a Japanese lantern and a straw mat. Some sheepfold!

"Just put up a tent or a tepee," Stewie snapped. "Call God from your cell phone! Or Shepherdess Moriah!" That woman had caused more trouble than he expected.

Ginger ignored him. She pushed a torn magazine page toward him. "We could build my sheepfold in the far corner of the yard, next to the rock garden. Next spring."

Stewie sighed. The rock garden was another disaster. Ginger lost interest when her expensive cacti died in the winter snow. Weeds took over and a stray cat birthed six kittens in the tall grass. Maybe she would forget the whole thing after the holidays.

Ginger rattled on, "I need a place of peace and quiet for daily meditation. My Angela Star horoscope said that I need spiritual nourishment."

"Try pyramid power," Stewie mumbled. Their new neighbor—who was exotic-looking with her paisley head scarf and crescent earrings—was into pyramid power. Said it did wonders for her migraine headaches. Ginger should talk to her. He said nothing more, packed his suitcase and headed for the airport.

He drove by the Sugar Maple, now leafless, a skeleton of mighty branches etched against the winter sky. The seasons went so fast, now that he was older. How soon would he become like the tree with wrinkled limbs and a twisted body, maybe in pain? Life was cruel.

Stewie left Ginger's house—and Ginger never let him forget that it was her house—to fly to Las Vegas. He lied to Ginger about leaving early because he had made plans with Samantha, newly divorced. They agreed to share a hotel room. She would play the slots while he set up displays for the sales convention. Instead, Samantha changed her mind at the last minute. She flew to Cancun with her girl friends to celebrate her new freedom. He wondered if she ever intended to go to Vegas. Would he ever understand women? He sure didn't understand Ginger.

Stewie slumped in his airplane seat. A plump older stewardess with long crimped hair and scarlet lips rushed down the aisle. A well-tanned steward followed behind her. They slammed overhead bins with quick glances at fastened seatbelts. They didn't even give out pillows anymore. His throat felt dry. He needed a shot of something. Even orange juice would help without those stale little pretzels. Stewie closed his eyes. Finally, he fell asleep after the kid behind him quit kicking the seat.

Stewie landed in Dallas, because the company travel agent booked him on a cheaper flight with a three-hour layover. He shuttled to another set of gates and walked the long concourse past the souvenir shops, newsstands, hamburger and pizza parlors. His feet hurt and his carry-on grew heavier. Airports were a mess with people bumping each other and those bulky auto-carts honking to get out of their way. Maybe it was an advantage to grow old and get a ride.

He found a seat against a back wall. Who designed such chrome and vinyl chairs anyway? It was a cupped form that only a monkey would find comfortable. People were sloppily dressed, rushing in all directions, staring up at flight monitors. He supposed they knew where they were going. He wasn't sure about himself anymore. That Samantha-business scared him. Was he getting too old for anyone to care about him? He wasn't even sure about Ginger. He turned off his cell phone. He didn't want to hear Ginger talk about nourishing her soul.

A younger athletic man—maybe mid-thirties—with a heavy back-pack sat down opposite Stewie. He leaned over. "My name's Chuck. Are you staying here awhile? I need to use the Men's. Will you watch my stuff?"

Stewie shook Chuck's hand. "Sure. I'm here for three hours. I'm Stewart."

When Chuck returned, he asked, "Where're you headed?"

"Las Vegas . . . a convention. And you?"

"Back home. Albany." He didn't say New York or Georgia. "I went to see my Aunt Beulah. I'm named for her husband Charlie. He made it big in oil wells. He built them. She's always been generous at birthdays. This time she gave me a check for a hundred bucks! Only a hundred bucks!" He thought a moment. "She's still after me to get properly married. I tell her I am married. I got married two years ago. Flew to Mexico. Right on the beach at Ixtapa. She says I'm not married because I didn't get married in a church. Even now, she wants me to have a church wedding."

Stewie raised his eyebrows. "I know what you mean. My wife's ex mother-in-law is religious, too—always after my wife and me to take the kids to church. I say that I believe in God. That's enough. She asks, *What does that mean?* I can't answer."

Chuck considered this. "We don't have to go to church to believe in God. Church doesn't turn me on. After Aunt Beulah's lecture on commitment. I told her . . . I don't need a piece of paper from a church to tell me I'm married. I already know that. I mean I'm REALLY MARRIED! My wife yaps about Friday night bowling with the guys . . . my shoes smell up the closet . . . my socks disgust her. Why do women change once they marry?"

Stewie thought about Ginger. Sometimes, he wished she WOULD change with her continual demands about redoing rooms. "My wife doesn't go to church, but she wants to nourish her soul. I don't have time for that stuff. I've got to make a living. It's crazy, but the more I make, the more I go in debt. You figure it out."

"Aunt Beulah says a commitment in church would be different from our wedding in Ixtapa. She says the vows we made were meaningless. She laughed at our promise to spend every anniversary watching a sunset together. She asked, *What if it rains*? She thinks we can't love each other until we can give up our own wants . . . like bowling. That's a bad idea. I've got a right to live any way I want. She said that I don't know a thing about God, either."

"I've heard that one, too." Stewie nodded.

"I said I could worship God on a beautiful golf course. Aunt Beulah snapped back *And pray for a hole-in-one*? I said I had a personal God. She questions me, *Do you think you can have God in your back pocket, and pull him out when it's convenient? Don't you really worship the holy trinity of me, my and mine*? She made me so mad, I quit listening."

"My wife doesn't listen to me. Even if she gets her meditation igloo, next she'll want a backyard pyramid or a bowl of crystals. She's tries everything. Nothing lasts. She's always looking. Her horoscope told her to nourish her soul." Stewie pushed down his anger. "Her ex in-laws said we would find Jesus'secret and learn how to live if we went to church. Well, Jesus didn't have a wife or kids. I don't have time for sermons." Stewie shifted uncomfortably.

That business about *knowing how to live* bothered him. Yeah, he had plenty of experience, but he felt imprisoned without the right combination to get out. Nothing made sense anymore. Wasn't it his right to have life, liberty and the pursuit of happiness? Life? His body was tired. He had heartburn a lot of times and took those little green pills. He didn't tell Ginger, because she'd come up with some cockeyed cure. Liberty? He wasn't free—not with the kids and Ginger. Pursuit of happiness? He tried to think when he'd ever been happy. Maybe when he was eleven and went fishing with his uncle and caught a walleye. So long ago that it was hard to remember. Was he getting forgetful, too?

"Aunt Beulah kept probing—*You say that you believe in God. Then tell me about him.* I didn't know what to say," Chuck admitted. "Then she zaps me with one last question, *How can you believe in someone you don't know?* I've been puzzling over that since I left." Chuck looked at his watch. "I've gotta catch my plane. Good luck to you."

Stewie watched him walk away. He sat there a long time and pondered that last question—*How can you believe in someone you don't know?* He didn't know if he believed in anything—certainly not in himself. Somehow life was passing him by. Maybe it was too late to find out. If he just had something to hold on to—*something* or *someone*.

BUDDY'S LAST LETTER HOME

December 24

Dearest Cheryl,

I just returned from Christmas Eve services. The Chaplain said that we should write to our families tonight. The guys looked at each other and wondered if an enemy attack will start tomorrow. It won't seem like Christmas if we are fighting.

We have a scraggly tree in our barracks. I made three paper ornaments and put Jennifer, Jeremy and your name on them. I think about the three of you all the time. I'm glad you're back in Whittimore near your folks, so they can help with the kids.

My Mom wrote that she and Floyd are well-settled in their mobile home in Tarpon Springs, Florida. She will fly out to Sun City West to care for my Grandma Kitt who has a terrible case of shingles. Please send a card to Grandma.

Also send a sympathy card to Irma. I remember my interview with Henry. Afterward, you helped me with my report. That was my lucky day—when you spoke to me. He was in a nursing home for a long time before he died.

My Dad also wrote that he's been assigned to a smaller territory in the western part of the state. Ginger and the kids are staying in Whittimore and he intends to see the family on alternate week-ends. I hope it works. Will you invite Lance to a sleep over once in a while? I worry about him. He needs someone to really care about him.

I really appreciate the letters from your Dad. It seems like he enjoys the change in his career. I never thought he'd give up corporate work. It's fine that he's using his talent for that non-profit educational foundation. It's funny that I never got to know him until we started writing after Nine-Eleven. Your Mom, too, has been good about sending pictures of everyone. You're still the prettiest wife a guy could have. And smartest, too. I know you'll do well in college. One semester down—only seven to go! Right on!

Since I've been overseas, I see life more clearly. You said that with all your Dad's corporate moves, you never belonged anywhere. It was the same with me . . . two nights with Dad . . . three nights with Mom. Back and forth. Did anyone really care where I was? It seemed that they wanted to be rid of me and get on with their lives. I have forgiven them. I hope you don't resent your parents. They wanted the best for you.

We're told that we're here to keep the peace and save our way of life. Do people really want peace? A lot of people don't like us. We get dirty looks and called names we can't understand. Somehow, we're the bad guys. It's dangerous work. If the enemy doesn't kill us, the land mines will. Even the native kids have guns. It's not easy to believe in peace.

Tonight the chaplain talked about "Immanuel—God With Us." He said that even when the Prodigal Son was in a pig sty, God was there with him. He said there are many rooms in heaven and there's a place for all . . . even for me.

I liked to hear that, because more than anything else, I wanted a home—a place where I belonged. I joined the army because the recruiter promised that I'd learn a skill. I wanted to get really good at electricity or plumbing or motors. Then when I got out, I'd make enough money to get us a place—a place of our own. I still want it to work out that way.

If I don't come back, please find a house. You have an artistic eye and can make it into a nice home. I want the kids

to grow up and say, *Our Dad was a soldier. He told our Mom to get us a home—a place where we will always belong.*
I never had that place.

Your loving husband,

Buddy

A STORY FROM *THE TIMES*

By unanimous approval, a gift related to the historic pioneer Sugar Maple was accepted by the Whittimore City Council on Tuesday night. The Franklin County Historical Society recently completed a month-long fund drive to raise $28,000 for the *Save the Maple* project.

A protective fence and plaque will mark the giant Sugar Maple on Pioneer Drive. In recent years, occasional accidents have threatened the tree, located on the thoroughfare's curve.

"Many stories surround the tree," commented Cheryl Phillips-Smith, Society archivist. "We hope citizens will share old photos and clippings about the tree. Personal stories are welcome, too, as oral history is important in relating the Sugar Maple to our citizens."

Phillips-Smith added that written stories and tapes will be kept permanently at the Boggs-Canfield Mansion near old Fort Whittimore Square. She recalled that her husband, the late Master/Sergeant Douglas "Buddy" Smith, Jr., asked her on their first date—the high school prom—at the pioneer tree.

She recently completed a Fine-Arts degree and is the new assistant curator at the Boggs-Canfield house. An exhibit on the Boggs sisters will be held soon and she would appreciate any artifacts related to them. Miss Lavinia's treadle sewing machine was found in the attic. The upright grand piano of Miss Rose has been restored and returned to the mansion by an anonymous donor.

THE END

www.ingramcontent.com/pod-product-compliance
Lightning Source LLC
Chambersburg PA
CBHW050349030726
47503CB00008B/2699